Charles W Jay

My New Home in Northern Michigan

Charles W Jay

My New Home in Northern Michigan

ISBN/EAN: 9783743382596

Manufactured in Europe, USA, Canada, Australia, Japa

Cover: Foto ©Andreas Hilbeck / pixelio.de

Manufactured and distributed by brebook publishing software (www.brebook.com)

Charles W Jay

My New Home in Northern Michigan

IN NORTHERN MICHIGAN,

And Other Tales.

—————:O:—————

BY CHARLES W. JAY.

—————:O:—————

TRENTON, N. J.:

Printed by W. S. and E. W. Sharp, 23 East State Street.

1874.

DEDICATED.

First—To Charles V. Mead, who, in the day of direst necessity came voluntarily to my relief, and positively refused all recompense, when, at a more fortunate period, I had the ability to evidence my honesty and gratitude.

Second—To the public, from whom I never received or deserved favors.

Third—To myself, as an egotist who attempted fame without stability of character, and succeeded only in achieving a questionable notoriety.

CONTENTS.

BIOGRAPHICAL.

THE average reader of those kind of books that are mainly founded on the personality of the writer, are apt to be curiously inclined to know something of the private history of the one who thus ventures publicly before them as a claimant to their favorable consideration. There is generally a feeling of sympathy with such reader toward such author, which strengthens with the progress of perusal, until it ripens into the desire of a more minute knowledge of the outer and inner life of him who has so interested them.

Knowing that this little book, the child of my later years, will be kindly received and welcomed by a large number of men, and a far greater number of women—the latter *always* permitting the flood of sympathy, in which eddies the worthless driftwood of "sentiment," to overflow the shallower depths of the brain—I proceed at once to unlock myself to all such as may be under the suggestions of curiosity, or the promptings of interest, for a glance or a stare at the "elephant," as he swings his inky trunk through the coming pages.

Like all truly great and eminent men—at least in this our own country—I was born "of poor but respectable parents." My father was a shoemaker, and waxed poorer and poorer with the yearly increase of his family, until he could hardly make both ends meet. His sole means of support was his trade, at which he hammered away day and night, in order to get the upper hand of the hard necessity that tacks'd all his energies. At last, by unrelieved confinement, he was assailed by a stitch in the side,

PREFATORY.

THIS is my first attempt at publication outside of the columns of a newspaper. Through a period of thirty years I have been connected with journalism in the city of Trenton, and have written more upon the ephemeral subjects of the hour than any other man in the State of New Jersey; and without boasting, may be permitted to say that but very few other writers have penned so little worthy of preservation. I wrote as the humor happened to direct or necessity impelled. Careless of what I said, indifferent to public opinion, reckless of the effect upon my personal interests, I "went in" on the Irish injunction of "wherever you see a head, hit it."

The natural consequence, of course, reacted upon myself. Talent, misguided, may be in demand when the temporary passions of the people blind them to the amenities of controversy, or the whispered monitions of judgment; but as the tumult passes, and reason returns, the champion of mere strife is weighed in a more carefully adjusted balance, and "found wanting" is labelled upon his merits. I know and feel all this, but it is a principle of moral law that the reckless man learns wisdom when it is too late to be benefited thereby. Whether this law is relaxed in individual cases, is just now a conundrum in which I have special interest, and the solution cannot be very far distant.

But to this book. I resolved upon it only a few weeks ago, and have written it without method or forethought, and with all the rapidity that I could draft into the service. In fact, it has been rather an effort of muscle than of mind, and a charitable judgment is invoked upon the result. Rude sir, or gentle madam, to be honestly blunt with you, the writer needed money, and as borrowing is "played out," in panic times, your servant adopted the only alternative that gave a faint promise of temporary relief. What little of pecuniary value remained to the subscriber in this world, went up in that interesting balloon, known as the Northern Pacific Railroad.

And therein rests the reason, explanatory of the fact of my charging so much more for this volume than it is really worth! When one has been badly skinned by reposing confidence in others, it seems that he naturally takes a sort of melancholy satisfaction in getting even by skinning everybody else who can be inveigled within the reach of his clutches. That's what's the matter with your author.

It is proper to state that a portion of my work in reference to Northern Michigan was written at odd hours for Beecher's Magazine, and is republished without revisal, and with all its imperfections as first hastily penned. Most of the other sketches were recently reeled off, and handed to the printer just as they dropped from the pen, without addition or subtraction. I know they are very imperfect, far short of what a purchaser has the right to expect. But I've got your money, and what are you going to do about it? The financial morals of the American Congress must be sustained by an enlightened and loyal constituency. That's the kind of a man I am!

As I said before, this is my first effort in the story line of publication, and written under the spur of necessity. And if the two love tales herein unfolded seem maudlin to the ancient maiden or the wrinkled beau, please retrace your own earlier days of romance, and remember that we boys will be boys, and that the love foibles of youth are the most pardonable in heaven and on earth, of all the weaknesses of our

poor fallen nature. Spinster of an uncertain age; beaux
rejuvenated by hair dye, and unhappy because December is
not June, relax the frown of jealous envy, and take a philosophic view of the antics of us youth !

A few words more, and I disappear from my introductory
audience.

There are certain smart fools, who appreciate sound better
than sense, who will be able to find a world of fault with
these unpremeditated compositions. Before all such, I kneel
in confession at the threshold. The writer of these pages
never studied grammar an hour in his life, and at this
moment does not know the scholastic distinction between
a noun and a pronoun, a verb and an adverb, a participle
and—and—that other feller of the parts of speech, whose
name I have forgotten. And the beauty of it is that I don't
care the flip of a copper for all such deficiencies.

> " What's all the learning of your schools,
> Your Latin names for horns and stools ?
> If honest Nature made you fools,
>   What's all your grammar?"

But I fear that this will be found too extensive a prelude to
the careless and indifferent performance that is to follow. I
only again exclaim, in the language of the illustrious Tweed,
martyr to spasmodic municipal virtue, " *I've got your money,
and what are you going to do about it ?*"

MY NEW HOME IN NORTHERN MICHIGAN.

FTER an almost unbroken residence of fifty years, by
birth and citizenship, in the State of New Jersey, on the
evening of the 13th of November, 1871, I turned my face
Westward to join my family in Northern Michigan, wife and
children having preceded me by a few months. Perhaps
there is no man, however stolid by nature, or hardened by
habit, who can release the ties of a lifetime, and bid adieu to
scenes endeared by associations running back to the earliest
recollections of childhood, without at least a momentary sadness shrouding all his thoughts, and recalling his moral
outlawry back to the comparative purity of earlier years. Not
being a preceptible exception to this natural law of emotion,
I admit, without moral reservation or secreted intent of
deception, that I turned my back upon the city of my birth
and took up the long journey before me, with not exactly
that alacrity of feeling that is popularly supposed to animate
the bridegroom on his way to a marriage altar, or his after
trip for a Chicago divorce. As the train lumbered over the
Old Delaware Bridge at the legal speed of three miles an
hour, I found that my heart was in rebellion at my self-
expatriation, and that a perceptible trifle of unwonted moisture
had welled up from some long-neglected spring away down
in the darkened recesses of memory.

But this effervescent weakness was not of long duration.
Sorrows of this nature are like those of childhood, touching
but brief; the sun soon absorbs the April shower. It has

been divinely and wisely ordered that pangs of feeling are not chronic; they touch sharply and depart swiftly; there would be small happiness in the world else.

At midnight the train that bore the undersigned and his fortunes moved slowly out from the depot of the Pennsylvania Central, just over the Market street Schuylkill bridge, at Philadelphia, and pushed on into the darkness upon its mission.

But fate seemed averse to my "new departure," and manifested her displeasure at my rebellion throughout the journey. While the glare of the city lights was still visible from the car windows, the iron horse balked, and notwithstanding the fireman "hauled him over the coals," he only continued to snort at intervals for a full hour before he could be goaded to his ordinary speed.

Lager is a great somnificator, and the undersigned soon faded away gently into the arms of sleep.

"Sleep that knits up the ravell'd sleeve of care"

is one of the few ancient institutions that has not gone out of fashion, and still maintains its original connection with its younger brother, Death, in the counterfeit business. Sleep pretends to be death, and awakes in this world. Death fools annihilation by leaping from the grave into the indescribable glory of eternal life. If this is a delusion, in God's name hold on to it! It never hurt anybody yet.

Early dawn found us entering the gorges of the Alleghenies. A furious storm howled through the desert solitude, and the lofty tree tops swayed to and fro, as if seeking relief from agony. On our right the beautiful but erratic Juniata wound its way towards the still more lovely Susquehanna;

and just here memory awoke as from a long protracted sleep, and unrolled one of her strangest pages for my perusal.

Nearly thirty-five years ago, ere I had arrived at the estate of a voting citizen of this great and greatly humbugged republic, I passed along this very spot, on the bosom of this very river, looking exactly as it does now, unchanged by time and its innovations. I was then on my way to Ohio, at that day a frontier State, with the great West beyond almost unknown, and a Pacific Railroad undreamed of, save in the despotic vagaries of Tom Benton. I had six silver half-dollars in my pocket, with two dollars' worth of wardrobe secured in a shilling handkerchief, and my passage paid to Cincinnati. A strong heart and willing hands were considered a good outfit for a boy-man in those days. It is different now.

The Juniata at that time was made tributary to the needs of internal commerce by what was called "slack water navigation." Dams were constructed across the river at intervals, by which its waters were widened out into ponds. From the canal our boat would be guided into these ponds, dragged along for miles, then slipped on to trucks that ran into the water from the railroad track, railroaded other miles, then again slid into the canal, then into the river, and so alternating to the end.

It seems strange to look back and see how we were carried over the highest ridges of the mountains. At the top of the ridges were powerful stationary engines. When our boat on the railroad trucks would reach the base of these steep elevations, a huge cable would be made fast to the head of the train, and the stationary engine would draw us up the dangerous steep. When we reached the short level of the top, the cable would be attached to the rear, and we would be let down on the other side by a like process. 'Taint so now! We go over and under, thread valleys and wind precipices, pass innumerable "dead lines" within an inch of eternal smash, and the traveller, unless he chances to look from his window, cannot tell if it be prairie or mountain he is crossing.

I remember one sight in that early trip over the mountains that fastened my attention so that it will be available unto death. The board shanties that enclosed these stationary engines just referred to, were fairly "papered" with the skins of huge rattlesnakes, tacked thereto by the attendants, who had amused their idle hours by capturing these interesting specimens of natural history. The exhibition fairly made my flesh creep, snakelike, then, and the memory of it now is not exactly a soothing balm to nervous inquietude.

As we descended the western slope of the mountain, fate renewed her attempts to thwart my purpose of leaving New Jersey to mourn my permanent removal from her territory. Our delay at Philadelphia had given an emigrant train the "right of way," and as this train had a trifle less than fourteen thousand Dutchmen on board, bound for Wisconsin and Minnesota, its headway was retarded beyond the usual dilatory gait of such lines, as governed by the "time table." One hundred and fifty miles east of Pittsburg we overtook said emigrant line, and were compelled to halt a full half hour to enable it to get ahead of the chances for a collision. A short run brought us again in view of our unwelcome consort, and another impatient halt was the result. And so we continued until we reached the doomed (I came near writing it d——) city of furnaces, fire, and bituminous brimstone, fully six hours behind time.

At 4 o'clock P. M., we started up the banks of the Allegheny river, crossed the Ohio about dusk, and found ourselves on a straight road running through a country of an almost unbroken level. A furious storm was raging, the rain came down in sweeping floods, and the winds raged with an incessant fury that found few precedents within our memory. About midnight, when everybody on board who had a good conscience was asleep, or should have been, fate made another desperate effort to stay my flight from the home and associations of a long life, and the despairing citizens of a sovereign and independent State, Tom Scott, and the fused monopolies of Camden and Amboy, and Pennsylvania Central included. She uncoupled the palace car in which I reposed in slumbering innocence, from the rest of the train, and the engineer being doubtless asleep, did not hear the parting of the bell-rope, and the speed of thirty-five miles an hour continued unchecked, leaving us standing upon the track with the hurricane howling for admission at every window! In about thirty minutes the engineer discovered his loss, and returned to repair damages. All hope of making up lost time before reaching Chicago was now abandoned, and the locomotive settled down to a less alarming speed.

We reached the charred ruins of the City of Divorces about noon the next day. As the Northwestern line through Wisconsin had left without waiting for our connection, we had five hours to stay for the evening train. I found it impossible to realize that the still smoking mounds through which I wandered were the debris of what, a few days before, was one of the largest and most enterprising and wealthy cities in the world. In an unbroken view of *miles*, scarce a wall was left standing. The long lines of former streets could only be plainly traced by the almost unscorched Nicholson pavement that stretched through the endless arteries of what had so recently been the proud and wicked commercial capital of the mighty and expansive West. Vast heaps of machinery of cunning skill and matchless work-

manship, now disjointed and warped out of all usefulness by
the destructive element that had tried it in the ungovernable
furnace of fervent heat, were to be seen on all sides. The
front of some of the principal blocks of stores could be
traced by the huge iron safes, that still rested, in almost
uniform lines, where they had dropped through into the
ashes. For miles upon miles all the more palpable evidences
of a great conflagration had been removed. Of the scores
of churches, whose vain pomp of architecture had so recently
mocked the manger of the founder of Christianity, the
ruined walls of one alone remained. The horrid gaps in its
blackened masonry seemed grinning in mockery of its proud
founders, and its steepled dome leaned dangerously from the
Heaven its pride had so recently offended.

Reader, your imagination is unequal to the task of fully
contemplating the matchless ruins of Chicago. Pen and
pencil, with their almost divine magic, are feeble here. Think
of *twenty-seven hundred acres* of crowded warehouses and costly
dwellings, filled with all the productions and luxuries of a
highly stimulated commercial civilization, reduced to ashes
in a fiery crucible—a hatful of alkali to each million dollars—
and you have the facts in a convenient compass for contemplation !

At 5 o'clock I started for Milwaukee. The track lies
along the western shore of Lake Michigan, that wonderful
body of fresh water that is more dangerous to vessels than
the Atlantic ocean, and whose wrecks are more numerous
than those of any sea in the world. We arrived in Milwaukee about 9 o'clock in the evening, and here fate made a last
desperate effort to divert me from the continuance of my
journey to almost solitary exile in the wilderness. A great
wind smote the lake, and the steamer dare not venture out
upon the turbulent waters ! I staid all night at the Kirby

House, an excellent Hotel with all possible accommodations, and kept by a fine looking landlord, and a gentleman of most courteous dignity of bearing. His name is A. Kirby. Fare only $2 per day. I paid my bill, so this is no " dead-head " notice.

Milwaukee is a city of ninety thousand inhabitants, seventy thousand being of German origin. It is situated on a high bluff of the lake and has a secure harbor. It is solidly and massively built of cream colored brick, and does an immense business in grain, pork, beef, and general merchandise, and is destined in a few years to become a great and notable city. And yet in 1840, Milwaukee was refused a post office by the government on the ground of not having inhabitants enough to justify such a favor! Think of this, ye dull natives of Trenton, and go into your holes! Your city is five times as old as this place in the wilderness of Wisconsin, and yet you have not stamina enough to build a mile of railroad, and you are without a hundred yards of decent street pavement in all your borders! Avaunt!

The Germans are a wonderful people in a new country. Democratic in politics, and jealous of the encroachments of government, these great elements of sturdiness in manhood and pride in citizenship, constitute the Germans the most desirable emigrants possible for a nation like ours. It was Western German patriotism that went farthest in the support of the government during the aristocratic slave-holding rebellion. Coming from a country where tinselled courts and sensual potentates absorbed the greatest share of the profits of honest toil, they could hold no sympathy with a treason that intended to perpetuate a like condition of things in a republican government.

It is a suggestive sight to stand at the depot and watch the arrival of the long lines of emigrant trains as they pour into Milwaukee. You see *thousands* of German men, women, and children, dressed in the loose, coarse costumes of their country, clamber down from the cars to await the next trains toward their destination. The father and mother have great burdens of bedding upon their backs, under the weight of which they are compelled to stagger. The little children follow after, each one with some household utensil in hand, silent, wondering and contented in happy expectation. And these people, dumb to our language, strangers to our laws and customs, scatter themselves into the wilds of the vast West, and in a few years hew out new States to brighten in our confederate constellation. May Germany ever have a free and full welcome to our shores.

The next evening, at 9 o'clock, I went aboard of the large and staunch steamer "Lac La Belle," or "Belle of the Lake," bound for the Michigan shore at Grand Haven, directly opposite Milwaukee. The boat was advertised to leave at half-past 9 o'clock, and I found about fifty strong and rough-looking men in the cabin, mainly wood-choppers, on their way to the Michigan forests to fell pine trees for the hundreds of steam saw mills that line the shore of the lake from Grand Traverse to Grand Rapids river, a distance of three hundred miles. But the steamer did not leave her moorings until near 1 o'clock the next morning. All night long a large body of men was engaged in rolling and carrying the cargo on board, until not a foot of stowage room remained. And even then thousands of tons of the produce of Wisconsin farms remained in the immense freight depot awaiting shipment. The destruction of Chicago has temporarily doubled the business of Milwaukee, and an immense amount of freight has been thus diverted from the Michigan Central to the Milwaukee and Detroit Railroad, on its way to your eastern seaboard.

The bell finally sounded its parting salute, the gang-ways were cleared, and we steamed out of the Wisconsin river into the seemingly limitless waters of the great lake.

Michigan is the most treacherous of waters. It covers nearly three times the surface of the entire State of New Jersey, and is as capricious in its moods as an infant. You start upon its waters under a cloudless sky, with a breeze hardly sufficient to stir the curls (false) upon the neck of beauty. In less than an hour you will see the wary mariner scanning a cloud in the west no bigger than a man's hand. It spreads with the rapidity of electricity, and the winds rush from their caves to sport with the wave and its wrecks. The vessel, which but a few moments before steamed along with hardly perceptible motion, now begins to strain, and groan, and plunge, under the torture of the aroused elements. Soon the cabin is a scene worthy of the admirer of the animate picturesque. Men, women and children are pitched from one side of the cabin to the other, and thrown about in a manner that would be most ludicrously laughable, but for the fact of there being no disinterested spectator to the performance. All are compelled to take a hand in the game; and the emptying of stomachs upon the floor, or into each other's laps, is the rule, instead of the exception. The cuss who could laugh at his associates in misery under such circumstances, must be a trifle Satanic in his humor!

The marine statistics of Lake Michigan for the year just passed, show disasters to over one thousand vessels. She rarely releases the dead from her depths of a thousand feet. Her fretted waters have neither tides nor currents, save such as her erratic winds bestow upon their surface. As I sit here now, writing, in my little log cabin, the wind blowing a partial gale, I can hear thundering surges upon her beach, coming in landward through the dark and dense forests.

But, on the occasion of which I write, Fate seemed to have
withdrawn further protest against my departure, and yielded
to the proverb that "a willful man must have his way." The
lake was on its best behavior, and but a gentle ripple disturbed its placidity. I lay until daylight upon the cot of
my state room, disturbed only by the melodious snore of the
burly bison of a backwoodsman who bunked above me. Once
I reached up and punched him in the side with my umbrella,
but the monstrous heathen only grunted an anathema, and
snored the louder! Pardon me, Rev. Sir, if I prayed for a
shipwreck to avenge me upon mine adversary!

At daylight I arose, refreshed like a toad under a harrow,
and ascended to the deck. The high sandy bluffs of the
Michigan shore of the lake loomed up dimly in the far
distance. A thousand sea gulls flapped their white wings
against the placid waters, or sailed in the higher atmosphere
above us. Far inland, out of the majestic forests of green-
topped hemlock and pine, the crimson heralds of the coming
god of day began to kindle their resplendent fires. I stood
for an hour upon the deck, motionless and entranced, at the
marvelous glory of the scenic solitude. The waters, the sky,
the forests, illimitable in all, made me a worshiper of God
and his universe, though I marred not my holy devotion with
outward sign. If this is "infidelity," let the votaries in
temples made by hands excommunicate me without benefit of
clergy! I have learned to stand most anything, for my
unworthy life has been at warfare with the most sacred
formulas that have become established in the minds of men.

About 9 o'clock we reached Grand Haven, a town of over
two thousand inhabitants. It owes its existence and prosperity to its lumber trade, and around and about it are thirty
steam saw mills, going night and day. The lake, here, is a

little over ninety miles wide, in a direct line to Milwaukee, and we made the distance in about nine hours.

I soon took the cars to Muskegon, on my way north to my new home. The distance to Muskegon is fifteen miles, and we made it in sixty-five minutes, the new track being in unusually good condition, and no one stoppage taking up more than fifteen minutes to let off a passenger! The last census gave Muskegon a population of six thousand and two, and yet the blackened stumps of the recent wilderness still stand thickly in her principal streets! Her saw mills are her only source of prosperity.

Here I took another railroad for White Hall, a town of eight hundred people, eighteen miles distant from Muskegon. The speed on this road astonished me, notwithstanding I had made one trip in my life on the Freehold and Farmingdale road, in my once-loved State of New Jersey. By fastening the vision firmly upon a tree, you could satisfy yourself that the train was in motion!

At the end of the first half hour I became alarmed, and suggested to the conductor—a gentleman in very thin legs and astonishingly large feet—that he reverse the cow-catcher to the rear of the train, for fear that a drove of cattle, that started from Muskegon a few minutes after we did, might run into us. The conductor looked me intently in the eye for a few seconds, with a gleam of pity in his face, and passed on with never a word. He was followed by a boy peddling prize candy packages to the credulous passengers. Taking it for granted that the lad was the inevitable newsboy of all passenger trains, and forgetting for an instant my change of place and circumstances, I requested him to bring me the New York *Tribune*. The boy started, slightly changed color, and responded with—

" The *what?*"

B

"The New York *Tribune.*"

The lad drew a long breath and slid past me. Two seats to the rear he met the conductor, and I heard him whisper to that functionary:

"That old feller over thar's crazy; he axed me for a New York *Trombone!*"

The conductor then recited to the astonished lad my suggestion about the cow-catcher, and after that the twain never passed me without a scrutinizing look, in which alarm was blended with commiseration.

White Hall found me at the end of all railroad connection with Northern Michigan. The region beyond is an almost unbroken extent of primeval wilderness for three hundred miles.

White Hall is upon an elevated plain, and the situation is a truly pretty one. Like all western towns, it is laid out to limitless expansion. The founders of these embryo cities seem to contemplate the no distant day when their now villages will rival New York and Philadelphia in population and wealth. Muskegon takes in many square miles, and the lots in its only business street are held at $175 per foot. And yet, in less than ten years from now, the valuable timber of this region will have all disappeared, and the decay of the town will then be as swift as its incidental prosperity.

The contrast between the lake shores of Wisconsin and Michigan are very striking. From Chicago to Milwaukee, eighty-five miles by railroad, are spread numerous beautiful villages, handsomely built and adorned, and showing all the comforts of Eastern civilization. The intervals are filled up with finely cultivated farms, with large and comfortable houses and barns. You cross the lake to Michigan, and it seems like stepping from civil into savage existence. The towns are simply lumber depots, without agricultural interests. The roads from town to town are only avenues forced through forests of unbroken solitude, with here and there the log huts of lumbermen, but no signs of agriculture larger than a patch for potatoes, or for corn sufficient to fatten the solitary pig of the wild settler. And yet Michigan is an old State, while Wisconsin but sprang into existence yesterday. The valuable lumber lands of Northern Michigan have held her back in the race of Western progression. Speculators have monopolized these, and labor has been diverted from the soil to the felling of trees and the sawing of logs. The few have thus become rich, and the many are the slaves of a system of labor that promises no benefits in the future.

At White Hall I hired a man for eight dollars to take me to my destination, twenty-two miles distant. We at once plunged into the depths of the hemlocks, whose dense growth and thick green boughs almost shut out the light of day. Not a bird, nor an animal, biped or quadruped, greeted our vision for the first eighteen miles. Then followed at intervals little clearings of from one to five acres, and the axe of the new settler resounded from the gloomy recesses of the forests in every direction. We had now entered the southern rim of the promising "fruit belt" of Northern Michigan, and the land of "great expectations" in the immediate future. About every mile opened to our view a little peach orchard among the blackened stumps, the trees of which had just been set out, and ground was being prepared for others as fast as the axe could dispossess the old forest trees of their freehold, for the benefit of the new delicate exotic.

And now from the lofty, broad and level bluff of the "Claybanks," the mighty lake breaks upon my vision, and its green, limpid waters seem rolled out to immensity. A sudden turn in the woods, and the majestic inland ocean is again eclipsed from view, but its melancholy moanings still

touch the heart and the understanding with a pleasing sadness. At noon the last mile was overcome, and on ascending
a high elevation, a clearing of forty acres, encircled by mighty
hemlocks of the growth of centuries, was presented to my
gaze, and in the midst thereof stood the little log cabin of
" My New Home in Northern Michigan." Johnny and little
Alice stood at the door, and, with the mutual exclamation of
" Oh ! here's Pop," ran out to greet me.

I found my domestic fortress in these inhospitable wilds to
be a cabin of decayed and crumbling logs, upon whose roof,
from the outside, I could " lay hands" without theological
authority. But my wife, who is an extravagant and preten-
tious woman, had, " unbeknownst" to me, and without
marital authority from the party on the other part, added a
$50 addition to the north side of our ancient and time-
honored domicil. This little exhibition of wifely pride and
womanly vanity has probably blighted my political aspira-
tions forever and a day. The less favored settlers have
booked me in their memories as a " rustikrat" invader upon
their simple tastes and habits! I came here with visions of
a future seat in Congress; but a woman has let Satan into
this paradise of anticipatory salary grabbing!

There is a little bit of romance connected with this cabin
of ours that will interest the general reader, and I propose to
relate it right here. About twenty years ago, when Chicago
was just struggling into cityhood, there resided within its
comparatively sinless limits a young man named John
S———. This young man had fallen in love with a young
woman of the vicinage, whose name is omitted by the gossips
of this legend hereabouts, and so, unfortunately, cannot be
embalmed in the immortality of this volume. For conve-
nience sake we will call her Mary, a name ever sacred in the
recollection of many of us. Well, in due time Mary accepted

the overtures of her impassioned lover, and promised to join teams with him in the burden of life. But even when the " happy day " was but a few weeks in the future, his affianced met a more attractively bedizened " feller " at a party, who wore "store clothes " of the latest fashion, gold rings upon his fingers, sang such affecting love songs as "Barbara Allen," " Lord Lovell," &c., and parted his bear-oiled hair in the middle. The young man thus endowed by art and nature laid siege to the heart of the simple country girl, and the garrison, after a feeble resistance, surrendered at discretion. In short, Mary "went back " on John, and was soon engaged to his rival. The blow staggered our hero beyond recovery. Like Hamlet, Prince of Dunkirk, he became morose, moody, and possessed of a melancholy that bordered close upon insanity. For days he walked about

> " With his doublet all unbrac'd :
> No hat upon his head ; his stockings foul'd,
> Ungarter'd, and down-gyved to his ankles ;
> Pale as his shirt : his knees knocking each other;
> And with a look so piteous in purport,
> As if he had been loosed out of hell,
> To speak of horrors."

Thus torn by the hopeless pangs of betrayed affection, he wandered one day down to the estuary of the great lake, just as a party of Indians, having disposed of the furs of the winter's trapping, were about to return to their lodges in the upper wilderness. He stepped into one of the canoes without a word, seated himself upon a pile of blankets, and bent his head in moody reflection upon his knees. The two chiefs of the red men held a brief consultation in reference to the silent intruder, which evidently resulted in accepting the situation. In a few minutes the elder in command gave a signal wave of the hand, the paddles dipped silently into the waters, and the fleet shot out northward. On the fifth day thereafter, several stoppages along the shore having been made to shoot deer and broil venison steaks, the boats reached. Petite Point au Sauble, one-half mile in a direct line from the cabin in which I now am penning this little episode of local history. The Indians, about thirty in number, had arrived at the landing place of their reservation, and at once began to unload the proceeds of their trading expedition. When the last package was removed, the leader of the band touched our hero upon the shoulder and motioned him to shore. He obeyed without a word, for he seemed hopelessly bewildered in mind, and as passive as a child. The burdens were soon strapped upon the backs of the Indians, the chiefs bearing their share with their followers, and the procession, in single file, marched up the steep sand bank that still borders the dense and sunless depths of pine and hemlock.

A march of twelve miles brought the party to the lodges of their tribe, on the spot now occupied by the village of Hart, the capital of this, Oceana county. Our hero remained with his involuntary captors for about six months, during which time, by his skill in the use of the few tools attainable, he constructed a new council chamber for the tribe, and a number of cabins for the chief men, of wonderful design and workmanship. At the end of this time he signified his intended departure. The tribe, (the remnant of the old and warlike Chippawas, and numbering about eighteen hundred souls), remonstrated in vain against this resolution. The chief, Big Bone, even offered our hero his beautiful daughter to wife, but the temptation fell upon unheeding ears. John came into the wilderness to get rid forever of the presence of the white woman, and the red one was not likely to win him from his general abhorrence of the sex. A wife! No, none for John! He was not to be Chicagoed a second time. The forest fawn of the lodge of Big Bone, whose feet were flat and broad upon the mountains, and in whose nose glittered the bone of the lake trout, plied her native arts in vain upon the petrified affections of our hero!

It was while the dogwood was yet in its second blossom, and the leaves on the maple had begun to crimson at the touch of the early frost, that John S—— strapped his blankets upon his back, shouldered his rifle, belted his axe about him, and, followed by the wails and supplications of these simple children of nature, struck out with long strides into the silence of the surrounding forests. He took the trail that led to Little Point Sauble, his landing point six months before. The sun, enveloped in his evening robes of gold and scarlet, with the encircling soft and fleecy clouds at a respectable distance from his more dazzling glory, was half hidden in the waters of the mighty lake, when our hero reached the rounded eminence destined to be so long his future home. He leaned his rifle against a huge pine of four centuries' growth, the sturdy stump of which still remains in the " clearing," three paces from my dingy window, mocking decay with its resinous roots. He next proceeded to loose his axe, and commenced lopping branches from a recently up-rooted hemlock. Of these he had soon formed a sufficient shelter for the night. He then made a healthy supper upon cold venison and parched corn, and laid down to a sleep that but few of the rich and great are capable of enjoying.

The sun, in russet mantle clad, had just begun climbing the heights of yon high eastern hill—[*Shakspeare*]—when our hero awoke. He offered up the first prayer probably ever supplicated to God in this unbroken wild, and then pro-ceeded to the new duties of life. Day after day he cut down the smaller trees, and fashioned them into the requisite shape for his proposed dwelling. The half dozen lumbermen then in this region gathered together to assist him at the "raising," and before the storms of November set in, John S—— found himself housed in a comfortable cabin, built by the labor of his own hands, not a stick or a nail of which cried out against the oppression or injustice of its founder. How many of your eastern " West End " nabobs, in their heavily-carpeted and gilded palaces, can show as clear a title to humanity and Heaven as this? Don't all speak at once. Lying is an abomination in the sight of the Lord!

And here, for nineteen years, lived honest John S——, at peace with his own conscience and his God. In due course of time, with hard labor at the saw-mills, which soon began to appear along the lake shore, he was enabled to purchase his forty acres, paying for the same the sum of $50. Of this he had ten acres cleared, a small peach and apple orchard set out and in bearing, everything around him lovely, and he himself, but for one corroding memory, a happy and contented man.

Just about one year ago, a change came o'er the spirit of our hero. A rustic ball was held on the 22d of February at the " Point," now a thriving settlement of four cabins and one " store." John was persuaded to attend. He entered the charmed circle of dancers with all the shy timidity of a youthful novice in the ways of civilization. When at last he lifted up his eyes, in the courage of increasing confidence, he felt himself entranced by a vision they encountered. There, fair, fat, and forty, but as pale as the linen that encircled her throat, with gaze fixed steadily upon his face— like one who has eyes, yet sees not—stood the beloved of his early manhood!

I am not a novelist, nor a man of imagination, but rather a sturdy delver in facts. Therefore, I propose to finish this true history without garnish or the gloss of improbable romance. As soon as his betrothed could recover sufficient self-possession for the effort, she crossed the room to her long-lost lover, took his hard yet trembling hand in her own, bent her head upon his bosom, and sobbed like an unhappy child. Of course, the wondering rustics were surprised at the strange scene, but had too much native delicacy of feeling to smile or giggle at that which they instinctively felt was sacred from vulgar comment and intrusion.

The explanation which finally followed elucidated the following facts: Mary, in expressing a preference for the "store clothes feller," and permitting it to be hinted among her associates that she was engaged to be married to him, had only indulged in one of those arts of coquetry with which so many young women foolishly try to test the devotion of the one they truly love. The sudden disappearance of her lover had awakened her to the wickedness of her conduct, and she had known but transient gleams of happiness since. A sister of hers had married one of a company of mill owners at the Point, and she was on a visit there when the strange meeting we have recorded was the result. The parties, thus strangely re-united after twenty years of silent absence, were married within the week, and that's the way our hero came to sell his forty acres, with the "improvements," to us, for the sum of $725, and departed with his bride to their old home in Chicago. Reader of "blighted affections," go thou and do likewise!

Having disposed of the preliminary journey and its immediate incidents, I now propose to convey my readers to the very ground of my new home, that they may stand with me and mine and take a view of the strange solitude and its surroundings. The location is called Blackberry Ridge, from the wonderful spontaneous growth and productiveness of that fruit in this immediate section. Our cabin occupies an eminence two hundred and fifty feet above the level of Lake Michigan, and is just one-half mile in a direct line from that wonderful and mysterious body of water. The moan of its troubled spirit goeth up unceasingly to the Infinite through these almost unbroken solitudes; and when the winds are loosed in their fury, the melancholy dirge can be heard for many miles inland. There is nothing that so lulls the soul into sympathy with eternity, and absolves it from unholy skepticism, as the voice of mighty waters in the waste and desert places. In this glorious wilderness, by the shores of this lonely inland ocean, not even the fool can say in his heart, " *There is no God!*"

The " clearing," on the western verge of which stands our cabin, comprises about one hundred and twenty acres. Of this we have forty acres. Two other cabins are visible, dividing with ours the cleared arena. Then we travel miles before encountering other settlers. My nearest neighbor, Charles Sessions, came in from the southern part of Michigan one year ago. Next to him is James Gibbs, postmaster, on a salary of $10 per year, and a Democrat. He came in as a lumberman about a dozen years ago, felled pine trees for the saw-mills for about five years, and when these were pretty well thinned out, Gibbs pre-empted a homestead of about one hundred and sixty acres, and became a " settler." He came from Pennsylvania.

The timber here is divided into what is called " hard wood" and " soft wood." The former consists mainly of beech and maple; the latter of pine and hemlock. All this region, for hundreds of miles, has been surveyed off into forty-acre tracts. But very few of the settlers own over one of these lots. All the land here was originally held by the mill proprietors, speculators from other States, who bought vast tracts for the immense pines which grew thereon.

These pine forests lined the eastern shore of the lake for hundreds of miles, and hundreds of saw-mills have been engaged in their destruction for the past ten years. The waste has been fearful. Between here and Chicago, a distance of two hundred miles, but few pines are left in majestic supremacy, the lordlings of the forest. For ten years the "best" have been annually marked by the spoilers, hewn down, and cast into the saw-mills. But the huge hemlocks have been passed by as worthless for commercial purposes. The new settler alone makes war upon these. They are yearly cut down by thousands, left to dry for a season, and then the remorseless fire is let loose for their destruction. I have seen acres of huge trees, most of them measuring from ten to fifteen feet in girth, set on fire and consumed that room might be made for the plow. There is a hemlock "forty" joining our location on the south. Seven years ago it was traded off for an old horse, worth $20. It can be bought to-day for $300. If you had it near Trenton it would be worth over $100,000. Next fall men will be engaged in cutting it down for the sole purpose of giving its beautiful lumber to the flames.

There is a singular feature in these forests of Northern Michigan. One forty-acre tract will be covered exclusively with hemlock. With hardly a perceptible gradation, the adjoining forty will be entirely of beech and maple. And so it will alternate for miles. The "soft" timber has a fertile soil of sandy loam; the "hard" has an admixture of clay and lime, and is considered far preferable for agricultural purposes.

On the west and south our cleared circle is girded by hemlock; on the east and west the hard timber mainly prevails. The contrast is very striking. The white, deep snow is encircled on one side by the denuded giants of the forest; on the other, the dense, dark limbs of the evergreens prevail

over all the changes of the seasons. I often wander forth of
a moonlight night—strangely brilliant in this latitude—
entranced by the magnitude and silence of these forests. At
irregular intervals, amid the leafless wilderness of oak and
beech and maple, rises up the majestic pine, straight and
limbless for an hundred feet, crowned with a feathery helmet
of green, and towering in altitude fully one-third above all
its surroundings, presenting a weird and ghost-like appearance that requires a more capable pen than mine to fully
portray.

The density of these northern forests is surprising. The
trees grow to an immense height, and so closely together that
the sun seldom penetrates their foliage. Standing in one of
these clearings, and scanning the outlines of the woods, the
great trunks seem so to press upon each other that one would
deem it difficult for a cow to force her way into their depths.
From these clearings one rides for miles, along narrow roads
winding among the trees, and filled with stumps, without any
signs of life or civilization. There is one road leading north
from this neighborhood, that can be traveled sixty miles
without meeting a human habitation. And this is the general
face of the country, clear across this secluded State, from Lake
Michigan to Lake Huron, and three hundred miles north and
northwest to Lake Superior. You of the old and busy east
cannot begin to appreciate the utter isolation and loneliness of
this vast region, or that sickness of heart that, despite his
philosophy, will at times overtake the voluntary exile from
an older and more seductive civilization.

It commenced snowing here on the 20th of November, two
days after my arrival. For six long weeks it continued, with
almost unbroken violence, and in all that period the sun was
not visible for two hours, put it altogether. Five feet of
snow fell in December, and violent winds raged without in-

termission. On the 16th of the month in which I now write (April) I came near perishing in a snow storm, having been overtaken several miles from my cabin. On Sunday, the 21st, another fierce snow storm was hurled from the heavens, and heavy icicles were formed at the eaves. One hundred and forty days of unbroken sleighing have here marked the terrible season, only now just fairly passing away. To-day, April 28th, the boys are plowing, with patches of snow still upon the fields. But there is a balm in the glorious atmosphere; the robin and the blue-bird are happy in our little orchard, and we live in a faith that tells us that seed time and harvest are not even here neglected of God.

But the ordeal to me this winter has been a fearful one. My life has been passed in cities and amid the tumult of men. For six months have I been imprisoned from all these, in a cabin in the wilderness, without one single link holding me to life-long associations. To step out from the rarely traveled road was to bury myself in the snow-drift. There was neither store nor tavern as a resort in which to relax the terrible monotony. There is not a single church in all this broad township of Benona, and not one drop of ameliorating whisky can be obtained for even " medicinal" purposes. The hardy pioneers here, who labor so hard and endure so many privations, are, with one exception, temperance men, and mainly members of the Order of Good Templars.

What I have carelessly written thus far has been at idle intervals, without any regard to the harmony of connection, or any caution against repetition. I had no thought of book making then, and since that weakness, against the remonstrance of judgment, has taken bankrupt possession of me, the assets must remain even in the condition in which they were found.

I have been very hard at work for a month past. My own

hands have cut, planted, and covered four acres of Early
Rose potatoes, finishing the unwonted work on the 5th day of
May. We have fifty bushels more to put into the generous
virgin soil of this yet untamed wilderness, and the ground
will be ready for the work to-morrow. Then come six acres
of corn, five of the little white beans of commerce, millet for
the kine, and many other things of minor import. To-morrow we shall finish setting out our thirty-acre orchard, con-
sisting of one thousand apple trees, three thousand peach
trees, five hundred quinces and plums, together with pear,
cherry, &c. We have been three weeks at this job, with a
half-dozen men to assist us. It will be a glorious sight in
a few years from now, when I am old enough to die, and life
has become a burden—which a sensible man would desire to
lay aside for the unknown future of eternal life or eternal
death—to see this thirty acres of red and white blossoms
blooming amid thousands of blackened stumps, and belted by
the encircling forest, giving its odor and its beauty from the
hand of God to the senses of man. It will seem strange to
most of my readers, this tale of southern fruit promise, away
up here in this northern latitude, by the mighty lakes, where
winter rages or lingers for fully one-half the year. And yet
there is no spot on all this broad country of ours where
peaches, apples, plums, strawberries, raspberries, and their
kind, come to more profuse and certain perfection than right
here in this circumscribed location of my new home in the
West—Petite Point au Sauble, running fifteen miles out into
the dark, restless, and treacherous waters of Lake Michigan.
Five miles inland these fruits, apples excepted, will not grow
to production. It is the milder influence of the immense
body of water by which we are nearly surrounded, that
makes this great difference of temperature.

My little cabin window, about two feet square, (blessed be

God, there is no worldly pride here to fret the souls of women and deplete the pockets of men!) opens upon a scene of sad and solemn beauty, which enlarges the Deity within us to an approximate comprehension of the Deity beyond all visible externals. The moon is full-fledged, and in this thin, pure atmosphere, gives out a resplendent magnificence upon forest and clearing that robs the sun and day of all their assumed superiority, and makes the dullest observer akin to the spirits of just men made perfect. O ye slothful servitors of Christianity, in the whitened sepulchres of your city Sabbaths, if ye would get nearer the Heaven you offend with your mockeries, and further from the Hell upon which your feet daily and willfully take hold, come out here and help me plant potatoes in the daytime, and worship the living and the true God through the work of His hands as reflected in the moonlight of these vast solitudes! It is so easy to be a Christian here that there hardly seems to be saving merit in it. If there be damnation beyond death, the city pursuers of wealth will mainly agonize under the inexorable decree. No man can be persistently wicked in the pure surroundings of Nature.

Seventeen years ago the first white man attempted a business residence on the lake shore, within many miles of my present location. Ira Minard, of Illinois, was the first to take advantage of the great timber wealth of this large county. He established a saw-mill at Stony Creek, an outlet of Stony Lake into Lake Michigan, about six miles south of my new home. A. R. Wheeler, of the State of New York, a very worthy and intelligent gentleman, was the agent of Mr. Minard in the enterprise. Roving bands of Indian hunters held possession of the country, and not a cultivated patch of ground could be seen from Grand Haven, one hundred miles south, to Grand Traverse, one hundred and fifty miles north. The second winter Mr. Wheeler was here proved a very severe one, and the solitary Indian trail that led to the trading post of Grand Haven was so blocked with snow as to be rendered impassable. Previous to this, the men at the mill used to make periodical trips to Grand Haven for provisions, returning with the same strapped upon their backs. On this occasion starvation threatened the occupants of the two cabins at the creek. As the dilemma became more serious, a trapper, a white man by the name of Chapin, volunteered to go in his log canoe to Grand Haven for supplies. He told Mr. Wheeler that if he were disposed to trust him with the necessary funds, he was willing to encounter the risk of the journey. The agreement was at once made, and Chapin started on his perilous trip. The lake was ice-bound for a quarter of a mile from its shore, and the huge waves thundered incessantly against this jagged and slippery barrier. Through dangers and hardships that can scarcely be credited, the dauntless hunter fought his way alone on the wintry waters to his destination. He procured ·a barrel of beef, one of pork, together with a quantity of small stores, and proceeded on his return. At the end of two days of fearful labor and peril, his practiced eye discerned a storm coming up from out of the west. He at once turned the prow of his canoe against the ice-barrier of the beach, and cut his way with an axe to the shore. He rolled his provisions high up upon the sand and entered the forest. With hemlock boughs he constructed a sort of shelter from the terrible storm that ensued, and rolling himself up in blankets, remained completely "snowed under," for two days and nights. At the end of this period, he regained his boat, re-loaded his provisions, backed out of his ice canal, and in a few days reached Stony Creek in safety, but in a state of complete exhaustion. Mr. Wheeler told out into the horny hand of the unselfish adventurer, twenty-seven hard silver dollars, as a reward for this perilous service. The hunter carefully counted and re-counted the dazzling coins, dropped fifteen of them, one by one, slowly into his untanned deerskin pouch, and forced the balance back upon Mr. Wheeler, absolutely repulsing all the efforts of that gentleman to induce him to pocket the remainder. Mr. Chapin now resides at Pentwater, twelve miles north of here, and has a comfortable home. He is a hale, hearty, honest old man of nearly seventy years, with no stain of meanness or crime upon his conscience. How would it have been with him had he lived in cities?

The success of Ira Minard, in the lumber business, soon attracted the attention of other men of resources, and mills gradually went up along the lake shore, at intervals of about a dozen miles, from Muskegon to the northern head of the lake, a distance of nearly three hundred miles. The land was held by the Government, and each mill company purchased thousands of acres, and the work of demolition began ; the glorious old pine forests, as old as the Mosaic creation, were assailed, night and day, by thousands of sturdy axmen, and scarcely a semblance of their former glory remains in all this region round about. The comparatively worthless hemlock, and " hard wood," have alone escaped this crusade of "civilization." Steam mills have sprung up in the wilderness further inland, and one of those near us has just completed a contract to saw seventy-five million feet of white and Norway pine for a company in Chicago. Three miles east of us, Kearswell & Co., lumbermen from Maine, hold twenty-five hundred acres of pine lands, now nearly denuded of marketable timber, by seven years of incessant assaults of hundreds of axmen. Their mill is a very large one, and chiefly manufactures what is here called "siding," but in New

Jersey is known as "weather-boards." The amount they annually cut up, with their marvelous machinery, staggers belief. A huge log is cast into the terrible maw of the mill, and in a few seconds the "siding" slides down an inclined plane, perfect for use. It is mainly shipped to Boston, and commands $70 per thousand feet. I wish my readers could travel through this wild region in the early spring, and see for themselves the *millions upon millions* of huge logs that have been cut down and "skidded," ready for hauling during the winter, and they would think that the whole world was being supplied with lumber from the forests of Northern Michigan.

The way this country was finally opened to agricultural attempts may prove of interest to my few readers.

The land was originally purchased solely for its pine. When denuded of this, it was considered worthless. The mill companies who owned it were from other States, and had no other interest in Michigan further than to despoil her grand old forests. Ten years ago the land thus despoiled was offered for twenty-five cents per acre. A neighbor of mine, William Worth, an emigrant from northern New York, was offered a forty-acre tract adjoining his homestead, if he would enter thereon and cut seventeen cords of "stave bolts" for the owner. These stave bolts are cut from oak trees, for the manufacture of barrels. Eight trees would have furnished the required number of bolts, and these trees could have been reached in any fifty square yards of the tract, and could have been got out in ten days. But the offer was refused. Another neighbor bought his forty acres for an old rifle, a powder horn, and a pouch of buckshot.

The original settlers were chiefly the lumbermen who came into the "pineries" for winter work. A few of these each season became squatters, and reared up little log cabins. They

worked at the mills in the summer to get supplies for their
families, and many of them plied the ax half the night to get
a little " clearing" around the cabin. Then, with a borrowed
ox from a more prosperous neighbor, perhaps many miles
away, they would break up the yielding, sandy soil, and,
amid half-burned logs and stumps, plant a peck of potatoes,
a little corn, a few square yards of garden, and trust to
Providence for the result. To the surprise of these first ex-
perimenters upon this seemingly worthless soil, the crop
proved astonishingly bountiful. For untold thousands of
years, Nature had been at work, in the air, in the snow, in
the water, in combining and secreting vivifying material in
the soil for the coming men, who were to make the wilderness blossom like the rose, and the waste places proclaim the
goodness of God toward all that trust in Him, and are patient
for his appearing. The field right here before my eyes, which
has been cultivated for seven years without return of manure,
and the half of whose surface seems taken up with huge,
charred stumps, last year produced two hundred bushels of
potatoes to the acre. Yonder hill top is luxuriously green
with its first clover, while the southern front of our cabin
holds a little orchard of fifty peach trees, which were four
years old last summer, and bowed down with fruit more
luscious than any that ever made a Jerseyman smack his lips
on Jersey soil. Every fence corner, every stump, every opening in the woods that admits the sunlight of the heavens, is
beautified and garnished with strawberries, and blackberries,
and raspberries, and their kindred fruits, lavish in unpruned
Nature with a profusion that seems like sheer, reckless
wastefulness ; for neither bird nor beast—and last and least,
man—can diminish by their necessities or gluttony these
healthy luxuries of our glorious northern summer by the
mighty waters of the great lake.

And the moral wants of our people are just beginning to be met. The first Sunday-school ever attempted for the neglected little children of the settlers was organized last Sunday. And who do you suspect is the superintendent of this Sunday-school in the woods? Tell it in Gath, publish it in the streets of Askalon! The superintendent is none other than your humble servant! How will that do for high?

It is night of the 20th of June. The moon is up in a cloudless sky, and the weary winds have retired to rest. The solemn religious silence of the surrounding forests is as pulse-less as death, save where the whip-poor-will utters his tireless and monotonous calls. And this lonely bird of the night stirs chords within the dim and silent wards of memory that have long remained untouched in the reckless past. It is now nearly fifty years since I last heard this bird of darkness and solitude utter its harsh commands to flagellate the offend-ing " Will," and well do I now remember the mysterious awe with which its persistent repetitions filled my troubled little heart. The scene was away up in northern New Jersey, and I was a little bare-foot boy, who gave his fond mother a world of trouble and anxiety. She is dead now, and that boy is growing old and weary-hearted, far from her grave.

"No more,
But let us to our story as before."

It ought to be of interest to all our eastern readers to hear how a wooded new country is brought under the dominion of agricultural man. The first settler generally comes out with an ox team, wife, and children. A tent is stowed in the wagon, together with axes, rifles, and a few positively indis-pensable cooking utensils. The pioneers travel on, days, weeks, and sometimes months before a location is selected.

Romance has no place in all their thoughts. Fertile land and convenient water are the paramount considerations. A spot is finally selected, and simple preparations for permanence at once entered upon. The tent is pitched, and the weary wife and lesser children are housed in their new home, in most cases never again to meet with those with whom all their years had been passed. The man and his stouter sons now select trees of suitable size, and for the first time since the world began to revolve upon its axle-trees, the startled forest is awakend by the ring of the woodman's ax. When the logs are properly prepared, the oxen drag them to the selected site, and by patient toil, and manly and uncomplaining privations, a rude log cabin—the forerunner possibly of some future Chicago—lifts its slightly majestic proportions amid its wild and primitive surroundings. The "squatter" having thus established his pre-emption right, goes to work with a will upon a "clearing." An athletic and tireless woodman can cut down an acre of trees in ten days. When a few acres have been so far subdued, the trees are left to season for a year, that they may yield the more readily to the persuasive influence of fire. Abundance of all sorts of game furnish food for the family during this period, a little patch of corn, cultivated in some natural opening of the surrounding forests, furnishing the needed concomitant of bread.

And here I will digress a moment to attack a popular error. It is an accepted untruth that the railroad is the one grand pioneer of civilization. Estimable old fogy of a philosopher, or political economist, stand up and be corrected. This little two-cent box of matches now upon my table is worth all the railroads ever built, or now being conceived, in wresting the wilderness from the dominion of solitude, and the silent reign of nature, and the grand majesty of uninhabited space. Fire, *fire*, is the monarch of civilization whose sceptre sways the earth, to say nothing of that other place that is theologically located a yet unmeasured distance beneath it. Not a square mile of wooded land in all the fertile sections of the great west and northwest could have been reclaimed for agricultural purposes, but for this subtle element, given unto us by the all-provident Creator. Let Tom Scott, and the ghost of Jim Fisk, make a note of this.

The timber thus felled is called a "slashing." When it is sufficiently seasoned, fire is applied, and then ensues a sight worth all the election bonfires in New Jersey. The wind is high, and the sheeted flame leaps and rushes like hell let loose for a holiday. Every leaf, every twig, every limb, every green bush, or creeping vine, that had decked or festooned the dead and prostrate monarchs of the forest, is lapped up by the hungry fires and consumed to ashes. With unsatiated appetite, or rather with voracity maddened with what it has fed on, the whirlwind of fire sweeps over the bounds of the "slashing," and rushes onward into the surrounding wilderness. The startled deer breaks from his covert, and the astonished eagle soars screaming upward into the heavens. And when night comes down upon the scene, it is only to add to the magnificent terror that seems a world on fire. Thousands of monstrous pines and hemlocks, long dead from the weight of centuries, but still erect by their firm fastenings—the skeletons of the forest cemetery—are seized upon by the insane fury of the fiery whirlwind. Up their huge trunks it crawls and leaps, and flaunts its lurid banner! It seizes upon each limb that seems to stretch forth its helpless arms imploringly. And now look! As far as sight can penetrate, here is a Saturnalia worthy of all the demons of destruction. The hoary trunks of the victims are all a mass of glowing fire, and every limb is ablaze with a brilliancy that fascinates the beholder, and throws an indescribable

glory by reflection upon all the surrounding green leafiness of
the forest. Hark ! Booming through all the avenues of the
intensified senses, comes a sound like muffled thunder. A
huge pine has yielded to fate, and falls crashing amid its
compeers. Millions of sparks fly upward from the fierce
concussion, and soar upon the wings of the night high up
into the firmament. And so, boom ! boom ! crash ! crash !
all through the night, at irregular intervals, the terrible conflict rages until daylight modifies the fearful and indescribable grandeur. I have tried feebly to describe what my own
eyes have beheld within a month past. I admit the failure
is a miserable one, and am willing that my enemies shall
make the most of it.

The fire of the "slashing" having fully exhausted the more
combustible of its material, the hardest of the work now
commences, for the "logging" is what the new settler most
dreads. The huge bodies of the trees lay prostrate amid the
ashy ruins and blackened stumps, the sole survivors of the
conflagration. These are simply charred around the surface.
The saw and the ax are now pressed into the service, and
made to perform their all-important part in the perfecting of
the work. The trunks are cut up into twelve feet lengths.
The log chain is fastened upon one end of these, and the
weary oxen are made to drag them to the place of execution.
By the aid of levers and "skids" these are piled up in
pyramids, frequently ten feet high. When this slow and
painfully toilsome process is completed, a favorable wind is
the opportunity for applying the torch. The numerous heaps
are soon in a bright blaze, affording a scene of grandeur at
night only inferior to the destruction of the lighter material
of the "slashing." The lurid fires light up the whole heavens
for miles around, giving an idea of the camp fires of an immense army. This work continues for days. Then the

windows of heaven are opened, and the dying embers of the
conflagration are slowly extinguished. The plow is next
called upon to perform its important functions. Where the
roots are lightest the ground is imperfectly broken up, and
the more delicate crops are sown or planted in little patches.
The potatoes are placed upon the unbroken soil, and covered
over with the hoe. The product of these is truly astonishing
in the yielding and congenial soil of northern Michigan.
From planting to gathering the first crop, they are frequently
left to struggle for growth, untended by the care of man.
And yet the production is often at the rate of one hundred
bushels to the acre, large, mealy, and of surpassing flavor.
I have been in twenty-five States of the Union, but never
saw such fine potatoes as are grown here in this wilderness.
God is good in some way to all manner of people.

And so, from year to year, the new settler adds to his
acres, until whole States are wrought out of the waste places,
and a sturdy race of honest and patriotic men grow up to
counterbalance the effeminacy and wickedness of the old cities
of the east. But for this, ruin and decay would have long
since marked the gradual downfall of our great republic.
There is to-day more of the leaven of national salvation,
right here by the lonely shores of the mighty waters of Lake
Michigan, than in all the borders of all the cities of the cor-
rupt civilization of the older east. The wild extent of our
country is the conservative influence that will save it from
the fate of the ruined dynasties of the old world for ages yet
to come. Poverty, oppression, and murderous discontent
have, in the yet untrodden fields of the mighty west, a way
to escape from enforced revolution, rapine, and bloodshed.

A painful incident of pioneer life happened five years ago,
right here in this immediate neighborhood. During a storm
a huge tree had blown down near the cabin of a settler from

Vermont. The next morning he took his saw, and accompanied by a little son and daughter, aged respectively six and four years, went forth to cut up the tree, which had fallen upon his crop in the edge of the clearing. He had sawed through the first cut, about twelve feet from the large space of earth that had been carried up with the roots, when the stump, relieved from the great weight of the body of the tree, sprang back and resumed its original position. The settler worked on for awhile, and then returned to his cabin for his oxen. His wife met him with a careless inquiry about the children. The man replied that he thought that they had become tired of playing and had returned home. The mother concluded that they had strayed out into the dense wood, in search of flowers and berries, and pursuit at once commenced. This was kept up for hours, when finally the alarmed parents instituted a closer search by the fallen tree. A loud shriek from the distracted mother brought the father to the roots of the tree. And there they saw horrible evidence of the fate of the little ones—the edge of a small apron protruding from under the re-settled stump.

The children had made a little play-house of moss and chips in the cavity caused by the uprooting of the tree, and when it sprang back had been crushed to death. The parents still reside here, and the mother has carefully preserved the little torn apron of her baby daughter, and the little straw hat of her darling boy, together with the withered grasses and wild flowers that had decked their play-house, as painful mementoes of their sad fate. I have seen them, and am not ashamed to admit that I paid unto these records of a painful tragedy the tribute of sacred tears.

There is a wonderful fact connected with the Michigan side of the great lake, that points to the wisdom and goodness of the Creator, in a manner so unmistakable, that it cannot fail to strengthen the Christian in his faith, and to weaken the skepticism of the honest and intelligent doubter.

All along the eastern shore, for over two miles inland, are steep and high sand-hills, studded with a stunted growth of pine and hemlock. These hills have been thrown up through the centuries by the action of the winds and waves of the lake, and being of more recent formation, accounts for the weak fertility of the soil, and the consequent dwarfage of the forests.

It would be a work of utter impossibility to get the valuable timber that grows beyond this belt, to the waters of the lake, over the sand-hills intervening, without an expenditure so enormous as to forbid the attempt for ages yet to come, or until lumber commanded a price difficult now to contemplate as among the possibilities of the future. Under this state of facts, all the vast region of which I have been writing would be useless in its timber for the necessities of the civilized centres in which it now finds so great and so remunerative a market.

And now I will show wherein the hand of God is seen, in the provision which so happily annuls the difficulty I have described.

At average intervals of about fifteen miles, all along our shore of the lake, little inlets enter the mainland, generally from one hundred to one hundred and fifty yards long, and from fifteen to thirty yards wide. Then their waters swell out into beautiful little lakes, which run up for miles into the valuable timber lands, and the most cunning engineer could not have designed these more skillfully for the great need to which they minister. These subordinate lakes are about six miles in length, by two miles wide. And all around the upper rim of this natural basin, large steam saw mills have been erected, the fuel for which costs nothing, and the lumber they yearly turn out is bewilderingly astonishing. An inlet, running from ten to twenty miles still farther into the interior of the pine forests, empties into the head of these smaller lakes I have attempted to describe. So you see that when the timber in the immediate vicinity of the mills is used up, a seemingly inexhaustible supply remains to be felled and floated down from a long distance inland.

The entrance from the great lake is dredged out to the proper depth, wharfed up on either side, and large schooners are thus enabled to enter, load, and depart to distant markets with their cargoes.

Additional force is given to the argument that Divine intelligence designed these marvelous conveniences for the benefit of man, by this other fact which I now introduce for the thoughtful meditation of both Christian believer and skeptical materialist.

On the opposite side, or Wisconsin shore, one hundred miles across from us, *none of these little interior lakes exist.* And why? *Because there are no forests of merchantable timber there that requires them for a highway by which to be floated to mill and market!* Reader, are not these links welded into the perfect chain?

While I think of it, it will be well here to introduce an explanation that should have come in some distance back in my careless and irregular description.

Some reader will think it strange, if my story of the general fertility of Northern Michigan be of a verity, and not of idle exaggeration, why is it that the land is not more rapidly taken up by emigration, and devoted to the general purposes of agriculture? Why does it continue almost an unbroken wilderness, while the colder and more inhospitable climates of Wisconsin and Minnesota are sought by the great army of emigrants?

The point is very properly made, but very easily removed. Of course the agricultural seeker of a home in a wild country is very limited in his means, and depends upon immediate crops for sustenance. It takes a term of years in Northern Michigan to cut down, burn, and get a forty-acre tract ready for production, and the cost per acre is about $30, exclusive of the original purchase. And then those wretched stumps last a generation, and are most difficult to work among, either in preparing for or gathering in a crop.

But the emigrant can cross the lake into the prairie states, enter government land as a homestead, or other lands at a light purchase, and clap the plow in on the very day he becomes the owner. Can't you "see it?"

To give my readers who are interested in things appertaining to my new home a compact idea of its wild isolation, I cannot do better than to state that it takes twenty-six counties to make up the population necessary for our Congressional District, covering an extent of territory much larger than the entire State of New Jersey, running clear up to Lake Superior, and bending around in a tier of northwestern counties to the Wisconsin line. Thank Heaven, it prevents any candidate from "stumping" it, or whiskying its wild red and white voters! His term of two years would be out before he could get through the district, and the "back pay" would be all stolen before his "grab" could come in.

There still remains in our county nearly two thousand Indians, the remnant of the once numerous warlike tribes that held all the Northwest previous to the inroads of civilization. They live on a reservation of two townships of the most beautiful forest land in all Michigan. It is covered by a growth of immense trees, mainly beech and maple, free from underbrush; and as one rides through it he cannot fail to become absorbed in contemplation of the magnificent profusion of flowers and foliage, so grandly displayed throughout this sylvan solitude.

These Indians are as good and peaceful citizens as are the white settlers, who are beginning to crowd so closely upon them. They have their little clearings for potatoes and corn, but hunting is the main object of their existence. They adhere to their old, original language, though the most of them have mastered enough of the English for the ordinary purposes of intercourse with the whites. The State prohibits, under severe penalties, the sale of whisky to these people, and to this fact alone is due their quiet and peaceable demeanor.

But woman will be woman, under all the dispensations of fate and circumstance; and dress without comfort, and adornment without taste, mark the sex wherever a mysterious providence suffers them to exist. The squaws of our lake region spend every dime they can get for three-cent finger rings, cheap, flashy ribbons, false hair not half so beautiful as their own, and hump the small of their backs as deformedly as do their Christian sisters of the East. In fact, I will dare the assertion that I have seen at least *some* red maidens here in the woods exhibit a disregard of taste in their attire equal to that of a New Jersey belle, in its monstrous departure from the true line of female development and shapely beauty. This may be doubted by most of my readers, but I stand ready to put up my money on it.

With the relation of a single incident connected with the present life of these Indians, I close this very hastily and very carelessly written sketch of " My New Home in Northern Michigan."

The principal chief of the Ottawas is one of the largest and most powerfully formed men I ever looked upon. His native name I have forgotten, but it is hard enough of pronunciation to strangle a Dutchman. He is designated among the white settlers as Louie General. This chief had a favorite pony of great speed, and his brother-in-law was the owner of a similar animal. Several trials had taken place between the two, but always with doubtful or unsatisfactory results. At last a day was fixed for a final contest, which the tribe attended in a body. These Indians are splendid riders, and racing is their favorite amusement.

This time the race proved decisive. The horse of the chief won the victory by a very close distance. This fact, and the vociferous yells which greeted the result, aroused all the vindictive passions of the defeated Indian. Instantly leaping from his pony, he rushed toward the horse of his brother-in-law, drew a long knife, and plunged it into the bowels of the panting animal.

There was a pyramidal log pile blazing close by. The chief gazed a moment upon his favorite, struggling in death, then with one bound he reached the offender, raised him in his powerful grasp at arms length above his head, and dashed him upon the burning pile! The top log, being nearly burned through, broke asunder, and the victim disappeared in an instant within the cavernous furnace!

For this deed of horror, Louie General was tried, convicted, and sentenced for five years to the State Prison at Jackson.

He had been incarcerated but a short time, when a conspiracy among the more desperate of the prisoners came to a head, in an attempt to overpower the guard and escape. This would have proved successful, but for the daring courage, and herculean strength of the imprisoned chief.

He threw his huge proportions in the only avenue of escape, and knocked down every convict who attempted the passage. Assistance soon came, and the effort was frustrated, only two prisoners having succeeded in making their escape.

Louie General was at once pardoned by the governor, and to-day is with his people.

HOW THE "OLD SETTLER" SETTLED MY POTATO BUGS.

I KNEW him by his swinging stride and his long rifle, the moment he emerged from the old Indian trail into the clearing.

It was the Old Settler. He came out from Northern Indiana twenty years before, as one of the first lumber camps formed in these wilds by the Chicago Saw Mill Company. He managed, at the end of two years' service in the camps, to get forty acres of land for about the same number of dollars, put up a little log cabin with his own hands, cleared off ten acres, and settled down in contented independence.

The honesty of this Old Settler would bear a heavy discount in any mart outside of Wall street. But there he would be sure of sympathetic and congenial natures. He is a Jay Gould, circumscribed in his genius by lack of material for extended operations. The first spring I came into the settlement, he sold me ten bushels of seed potatoes, at double the market price, every one of which was frozen to the hardest possible solidity. When a week later I discovered this fact, and suggested that he make some sort of reparation, he indignantly remarked:

"Why, stranger, do you take me for a durn'd fool! I'm a poor man. You wear store clothes and keep hosses, and they say hereabouts that you are lousy with greenbacks. But you musn't go for to try to put on style among honest folks here in the woods. Pay you back that money! Not if this indi-

vidual knows hisself. Who can best afford to lose them
'taters, me or you? When I was up on the Manistee last
winter, a loggin', I licked a feller about your size, with one
hand tied behind me."

The logic of these remarks would not bear close criticism,
but the huge fist which the speaker swung around, in rather
careless proximity to my head, by way of emphasis, had a
mollifying effect upon my anger. I assured him I was
only joking. The Old Settler magnanimously accepted the
apology, invited himself to dinner, borrowed three dollars to
pay his taxes, and struck out again into the forest. And now
he visits me regularly, and in the absence of all neighborly
companionship, he is at times rather welcome than otherwise.

When the snows had all melted last Spring, and had
poured the last of their tributes into the treasury of the great
lake, and the genial days came out from the shadow of the
long, fierce winter, I set about my innocent agricultural
labors.

Albeit of an indolent organization, and a dreamer rather
than a laborer in the great problem of life, still I find
myself, in my new mode of existence, compelled to work in
self-defense. There is neither store, church, nor tavern, nor
any of the accessories of civilization within many miles of
my lowly dwelling. The winds sigh mournfully through
the forests; day unto day and night unto night speaketh a
voiceless language of the past, in the solemn loneliness of
these grand old woods. The sounds of labor are few and far
between, and seem but the muffled echoes of the general
silence.

To avoid the saddening thoughts of death and eternity,
which such surroundings force upon the meditations of one
accustomed all his life to the remorseless din and struggles of
great cities, I went to work like another Abel, who was a

D

tiller of the ground long before the ornamental potato bug was mercifully invented. I prepared an acre for early rose, cut, planted, and covered six bushels thereon, and all with these soft hands of mine. The very first forenoon of this work satisfied me that I was the discoverer of a valuable acquisition to medical science. There is some secreted virtue in a Northern Michigan hoe handle, that raises blisters in a few minutes, as large as life, and twice as natural.

Rapacious quack, I have patented the discovery. The subscriber is too smart a Jersey Yankee to make public " a great blessing to mankind," without the preliminary caution of securing the profits.

Well, to make a short story long, my potatoes grew up out of the furrow, drank in the air and the sunshine, and I was happy in the consciousness of rewarded skill and industry. No fond mother ever so watched over the dawning beauty of her first-born, as did your servant, beloved reader, over the developed glory of them 'taters! Alas, for the cruel sequel! One day

> The bugs they came down, like wolves on the fold,
> And eat of my vines all their stomachs could hold !

It was at this fatal juncture that my evil genius, the Old Settler, emerged from the forest, and came upon the scene, as related at the opening of this history. Coming up to where I was sitting moodily upon a stump, feeling like Marias at the ruins of Carthage, only more so, his keen eye took in the situation at once, but his diplomatic caution suggested the disguise of an inquiry :

" What mout the matter be ?"

" Look at what was, only yesterday, the most beautiful potato patch in the settlement. In forty-eight hours from this it will be a sandy, herbless waste."

" Bugs, eh ?"

" Yes."

" Is that all ?   Why, stranger, you can kill every blasted critter of 'em, sure as shootin', before 9 o'clock to-morrow mornin'."

In the hour of despondency, the feeblest support gives hope a ray of confidence.   I grasped with gratitude the hand of the Old Settler, and eagerly inquired how the work of extermination could be effected.

" Mister," said he, " you're a new beginner, and don't know much about farmin'.   But you're a clever feller, as far as *I've* seen, and I'm willin' to give you my 'sperience.   Go and get a bushel of fresh lime, what's just outen the kiln.   Pound it up as fine as powder, and early in the mornin', when the dew is thick, dust them are vines all over, and by noon there won't be a durn'd live 'tater bug in the hull patch."

With a gush of feeling that uprooted all my previous pre-judices, and flushed tearfully in my eyes, I again grasped the hand of the kindly old man, with a mental oath of eternal friendship; hitched up " Prince," and drove like Jehu, the son of none, to Stony Creek, eight miles distant; got back at dusk with the lime, and worked and sweated all night in reducing it to powder.   I stole out exultingly in the early grey of the morning, and gave a magnificent dusting to the whole patch !

My triumph was of the kind supposed to be loved by the gods, for it died young.   Even as I waited and watched, the dust began to seethe and bubble, and a smoke steamed up, and the vines squirmed, and writhed, and soon lay prone upon the ground !

" Fine arternoon," exclaimed the Old Settler, as he strode into the patch where I was contemplating the ruins.

I looked in the man's face sternly for a full minute, expecting to see him quail in the consciousness of guilt, in full sight of the injury he had done me. But the steel blue of his eye remained unclouded with shame, as he observed, in a satisfied tone:

"Well, stranger, you see the lime has cleared the kitchen. Bugs all dead, I b'lieve?"

"Yes," I bitterly rejoined, "and *vines*, too. Did you know it would kill the vines?"

"Why, of *course* I know'd it would kill the 'taters. Any durn'd fool, who had the sense he was born with, oughter to know *that! But then look at the satisfaction of carcumwentin' the cussed bugs!*"

I here tightened my grasp upon the hoe handle, set my teeth hard, and breathed determinedly. But a spirit of Christian forbearance came in time to save me from the contemplated violence. I thought of the feller he had licked up on the Manistee, and grinned horribly a ghastly smile as I lifted my eight-dollar beaver from my head, and handed it to the Old Settler with a bow, and the exclamation of—

"Take my hat!"

To my surprise and consternation, the matter-of-fact nature of my tormentor seemed to take the offer as of good faith, and as a reward for acceptable service rendered! He stretched forth his long muscular arm, and before I could withdraw the offer, he had it safely in hand. He then lifted his own rimless, greasy, dilapidated "slouch" from his head, tucked it under his arm, put my "pride of New York" on his shaggy nob, and looked happy. He soon took it off, examined with pride and satisfaction the beautiful finish of the interior, replaced it upon his head, and spoke thus:

"Thank you, mister. This is the fust present I've had this many a year. Some of the folks here in the woods think you are a man of too big feelin' for sich as us. I've always found you to be a clever feller, without a bit of the gentleman about you, and I'll stand up for you while there's a hemlock tree on Point Sable, or a ten-pound pickerel in Bear Lake."

Thus leaving his sense of gratitude to console me in his absence, the Old Settler struck out toward the forest, in the direction of his cabin. On reaching the top of the hill, he halted for a moment, again removed *my* new hat, again scrutinized the beautiful interior, smoothed the body affectionately with his coat sleeve, replaced it, and was soon lost to sight, and not particularly dear to memory.

THE FIRST DEATH IN OUR LITTLE SUNDAY SCHOOL.

H E was such a very little fellow, and so delicate in appearance, and so bright, and kind, and gentle, and loving, that I first wondered how it happened he was a boy. As this conundrum was insoluble in human philosophy, I next spurred my ethical curiosity into another phase of unprofitable speculation.

"Why was a man child—so etherial—so good—so almost angelic in soul and body—permitted to be born in a cold, inhospitable wilderness, where mortals of the coarsest and the hardiest texture, who had never known luxury, and in consequence felt not its privation, alone could live without bemoaning a fate only preferable to exile, or involuntary imprisonment?"

This surmise, after turning it around into all moral aspects possible to an acute imagination, also eluded a satisfactory verdict, and was dismissed on its own recognizance.

The plain, hard fact alone remained, clearly defined upon the background of impertinent causality, that little Johnny Errickson, first son to a rude Norwegian emigrant, had been born, five years before my advent in that region, in a primitive little log cabin, on the eastern shore of Lake Michigan, and that an old Ottawa squaw did the midwife honors on the occasion.

And Andrew Errickson, the father, was killed on the morning of that same day by the vengeful limb of a patri-

archal pine tree he had mercilessly hewn down for the maw
of a saw mill. It was believed by the few white settlers of
the vicinage, that the sad fate of the father had hastened the
advent of the infant some weeks in advance of the natural
law in such cases made and provided. The shock to the
mother, so suddenly and tragically bereft of her young
husband, and left alone among strangers in a strange land,
is supposed to have forestalled the event in manner as here
written.

Be that as it may, the hard fact remains, that the dead
father and the new born nurseling lay upon the same bed
on the morning of the funeral.

That little Johnny was thus hastened into this breathing
world, may account for that nervous delicacy of organization
to which I have referred, and the manifestation of which
wrought within me such a painful and ever pressing interest
in the child, when I had learned the simple facts of his brief
being.

When we organized our little Sunday School here in the
forest, on a bright Sabbath in June, 1872, Johnny and his
mother made two of the nine human creatures in attendance.
The wicked writer of this was made superintendent, and his
Christian wife was the only teacher, a position which she
holds unaided to this day, January 1st, 1874.

Johnny was but five years of age; and I never looked
upon those great blue eyes, so full of strange, wondering
inquiry, and that thin, pale face, in which the dark veins
were so plainly visible in all their tracery, but the conviction
came uppermost that his little life would be but a brief
exhalation of its morning.

Of course the child could not read when we opened our
little Sunday School by the waters of the lonely lake, in the
faith that it would in time become as the voice of one crying

in the wilderness, "Prepare ye the way—make His paths straight!"

But he became a scholar, walking a long way through the thick woods every Sabbath, never failing to be present until—*he died!*

It was wonderful to see how intensely the little fellow devoted himself to his letters, and how soon he mastered them. I really don't think it was over eight weeks before the pale, sad-faced child recited to us, scarcely missing a word, the whole of the Lord's Prayer. And after that a Sabbath never passed in which he did not give us a half dozen verses from some portion of the Scriptures. And how his little face beamed with joy, and happiness, and all that sort of thing, when our commendation rewarded his proficiency!

The widow and her son were very poor, and Johnny would pick berries in their season, and carry them to the lumber camps for sale, and then run back through the forest path, as fast as his little legs could carry him, to give his mother the few pennies he had thus gained.

I remember one Saturday afternoon in the early summer of last year, that Johnny went down to the saw mill at the Point, with his little basket filled with wild strawberries, to dispose of to the hands. As he was about to return, the proprietor, a coarse, bluff, but kindly man, chanced to come out of his cabin, and meeting the lad, accosted him thus:

"Hello, Johnny, you're the very boy I wanted to see! I expect some company to-morrow, and I want you to get up early in the morning and pick me five quarts of strawberries. I believe you're an honest little chap, and I've got a new silver quarter of a dollar in my pocket, and I will pay you right now in advance."

The eyes of the child glistened with delight, and in his

excitement he threw down his basket, as though it encumbered his movements, and ran with all his might toward the outstretched hand that held the shining treasure.

It was doubtless the first silver coin the poor boy had ever seen, but it had hardly touched his eager palm, when the sunshine went out of his face, and his eyes were suffused with tears. The flash of a sudden thought had wrought the change.

He held out the bright temptation toward the hand from which he had just received it, and said:

"No, sir; I cannot pick berries to-morrow. It is Sunday."

"Why, Johnny," exclaimed the mill owner, with a laugh, (for no one had respected the Sabbath in those parts, up to the time of our little school,) when did you get this foolish thing in your noddle? Last summer you used to pick us berries every Sunday, and nobody ever thought anything of it."

"Yes, sir," said the child, "but I didn't know it was wicked then. But I go to Sunday School now, and can read, and the Bible says we must remember the Sabbath day to keep it holy."

"Nonsense," said the man, in a slightly impatient tone, "don't let those folks who have come in here from the East put such stuff in your head. Johnny, your mother wants this money bad enough, and it is your duty to earn it for her, Sunday or no Sunday."

A hesitating look began to creep into the child's face, for the man refused to receive the money back.

The boy was thinking of his mother. The contest went on.

The struggle seemed unequal, with hard poverty and a

little child on one side, and what appeared to his young eyes
as wealth on the other.

"*Not by power, nor by might, but by my spirit, saith the
Lord!*" The hesitation of the child was but momentary.
He dropped the coin in the sand at the feet of the tempter,
recovered his basket, and struck into the dark woods on his
homeward path as fast as his little legs could carry him.

He seemed to feel the danger of looking back. Reader, take
warning!

And this was the first visible victory of our little Sunday
School in the wilderness. Let strong Christian men and
women never forget the day of small things.

I think I told you in the beginning that this child must
die—that his brief dark morning would be his all of life.
It is the coarse and the brutal who live out all their days.
This is true. And yet, perhaps, it were better had I left it
unwritten here.

In the early September the dreaded scarlet fever, so fatal
in our high latitude, pushed its annual visitation into our
secluded settlement. Nearly all who were smitten died.

It was Sunday, and one of those soft and beautiful days
that are only in the fullness of their glory in the solitude
of the untrodden places. Johnny Errickson came not to
school.

And then I looked at the little bench on which the child
used to sit, his pale lips moving over his lesson with a
nervous intentness painful to behold, and I knew that his
place would know him no more forever.

When the night came, and the voice of the whip-poor-will
was alone heard in the silence, I started for the cabin of the
widow, which was about two miles distant.

I found three or four hard featured men, and about the
same number of uncouth but tearful women present when I

lifted the wooden latch and entered. The little sufferer lay tossing upon the bed, starting occasionally from a half doze, and throwing his arms about wildly. His face was scarlet, and swollen. His mother sat by the bedside, her face buried in the clothes. She was silent, but her heart-beats were audible to those nearest her.

At last the child feebly raised his head from the pillow, and said :

" Mother, it is all dark. Let me take hold of your hand."

The widow took the child's hand in her own, and the hot tears dropped, one by one, upon it.

"Mother, what makes you cry so," said the child, hoarsely. " God won't let me die, mother ; I am so little."

He laid down his head again, and for a few moments was so still that we thought he had gone to sleep.

Suddenly he opened his eyes, a glad smile was upon his face, he clapped his thin hands two or three times together, and exclaimed :

" O, mother, it is all light again now ! And see ! the room is full of dear little children, all dressed in white ! We will have a bigger Sunday School now, mother—O! ever so much bigger—won't we, mother ?"

Tears rolled down the cheeks of every man present, and the suppressed sobs of women filled the room.

The sufferer was again silent, but I knew by his shortened breathings that Death had entered the room, and that his skeleton hand was outstretched for the child's life.

Five minutes had elapsed, and the boy still remained motionless. His breathing became more and more feeble.

All at once he turned over on his side toward his mother, opened his eyes slowly, and with an effort. Then, with a faint smile upon his face, he whispered :

"Mother, your little boy's work is all done, and now he is tired, and will go to sleep."

I stepped softly to the bedside, and bent over the boy. His eyes were still open, but the life had left them. The spirit of little Johnny Errickson had passed over the dark river into the beautiful land of everlasting love.

I turned to the mother, and said:

"It is best as it is. Johnny is dead."

A wail of agony went out of the heart of the mother, as she knelt down and kissed the brow of the dead.

He was her only son, and she was a widow.

Then came a voice that was softer than silence, and said, *"Suffer little children to come unto me, for of such is the Kingdom of Heaven."*

DARWINISM VINDICATED AND CONFIRMED.

I HAVE always thought, since my giant intellect became more gianter by study and observation, that the Bible account of the creation of man was too absurd a tradition for any mind that had outgrown childish credulity, and laid aside its infantile books about Jack and his Bean-pole, and kindred stories, with which our good grandmothers used to win us to their feet, in the almost forgotten winter evenings of the long ago. But in the absence of any counter-convincing theory, emanating from a philosophic mind of unquestioned acuteness, and of moral respectability, I was compelled to keep ignoble silence upon a momentous subject that I could not credit, and yet unable to controvert.

The conscientious reader—he who desires to believe right upon a great religious question, and yet has no *philosophic* evidence to point the way from doubt into belief—can alone appreciate the joy that kindled its radiant delight in my soul, when Charles Darwin appeared with his monkey before the footlights, and holding it up by its prehensile tail, exclaimed to his audience:

"*Behold one of your intermediate ancestors ! ! !*"

To say that I was delighted beyond all facility of expression, at this happy solution of the question that had so troubled me for years, is but a feeble way of announcing the satisfaction I derived in thus being able to claim the cunning little creature of the primitive village show tent as a man and a brother!

Pecuniary considerations, of too delicate a nature for more explicit public explanation, alone restrained me from the immediate purchase of the coveted volumes in which the monkey idea was so fully and so satisfactorily elucidated.

But I was so fortunate one day, during an idle visit to that pernicious school of theological superstition, the "Young Men's Christian Association," of the city of Trenton, to pick up a newspaper, and therein I read an extract from the Book of Darwin, in which it was shown that man was developed, through ages of progression, from a rather shaky sort of jelly at the bottom of the ocean! This watering of our common stock proved the genius which conceived the idea, and has ever since found industrious imitators, of which the late James Fisk, and his worthy living executor, Jay Gould, are the happiest exemplars.

Finding that the water cure had drowned out the Bible fallacy of the "dust of the earth," in regard to the "origin of our species," I had a foundation upon which to rest my own lever, for the further overturning of the delusion of the pious, and misplaced faith of the weak and credulous.

And so I set my own active and investigating mind to the task of discovering cumulative testimony to brace, with additional strength, the theory that seemed so firmly based upon the great original principle of jelly.

The first thought that came to my assistance was one that might have escaped ordinary observation, because it was right under the nose, instead of being reachless, under the great depths of the ocean. The philosophic Darwinian, as a rule, is apt to despise the surface, and boldly dives to where there is neither seeing nor hearing. The dullest delver can grasp superficial facts. The real Darwinian brushes such aside, and with his long oyster tongs, dredges up the jelly from the bottom. I am but a freshmen of the class, a neophyte for the honors, and this is why I stood at the vestibule of science, and picked up the crumbs that had been swept out, unrecognized, from the Darwinian table.

But to the thought from which I am beginning to stray. In one of the instructive books of Charles Dickens, there is a person named *Jellyby*. How came that person so named, and what is the inference of her ancestry? The intelligent reader at once anticipates the point. The original progenitor of the Jellybys was, in all probability, the first of the human species! Developed from a jelly—what more natural than that he should name himself after the element of his origin? This deduction is irresistible—as much so, let me diffidently add, as any drawn by the great mind of which I am only a disciple.

In further pursuance of this logical train of reasoning, I remembered that Shakspeare, who comprehended every phase of human nature, describes one of his characters as almost

"Distilled to *jelly* by the act of fear."

This proves that the developed man was so frightened that he was almost dissolved back to his original elements!

And again—Why, when people become emaciated and weakened by dangerous illness, is *jelly* given to them as food appropriate to such feebleness? Because it is drawing from the *fount* of life to *renew* and *strengthen* the *decline* of that life!

These few incidents must suffice for the special point of illustration in view. Space, and not lack of material, demands this brevity. And now for the positive and tangible facts that settle the question beyond controversy or criticism.

Man stands with one foot upon the bottom of the ocean, and the other upon the surface of the earth, as developed from a jelly to a human being. Now mark how, by easy stages, the wonderful transition was effected.

We will assume that the first stage was from a jelly to a clam. Hence the origin of the word *clamorous,* when we become impatient for a result. Then the jelly-clam, beginning to get the hang of the thing by a dimly developed instinct, or mind, took a more lively stride, and clamed its way into a crab, thus advancing towards its perfect state, as a creature that can live both upon the water and the land. In support of this changed state in the progress of development, I need only adduce the fact, that in the language handed down to us from the remotest antiquity, a man with a contradictory nature is said to be at times a "little *crabbed!*"

And now the jelly-clam-crab takes a rather wider departure, according to his increased strength and intelligence, crawls forth upon the land, and suns himself as an alligator!! Hence it is that the proud son of Kentucky, impelled by an instinct without scientific knowledge, proclaims himself, "half horse and half *alligator!*"

But it is unnecessary to prolong these facts by furnishing the additional links that connect man with his creator, the gelatinous substance that oozes from the bed of the ocean. He who denies the Darwinian truths I have already advanced, would not believe though one arose from the asylum.

I am not disposed to rest here, however, for there is another field in the philosophy of development, that even the acute mind of the author of the "Origin of the Species" has failed to discern. I mean the origin of the celestial bodies. It may seem like ingratitude for a student to outstrip the master to whom he owes so much, but the claims of science are superior to the conventional requirements of friendship.

"How came the stars of the firmament in their exalted places, and the sun as master of the celestial situation?"

I answer this seemingly triumphant conundrum, with a single word :

LIGHTNING-BUGS!!

In the beginning a sufficient number of these wonderful insects were commanded to develope, to attain the grand purpose contemplated by Nature. The first stage of progress was those false meteors that occasionally blaze in the lower firmament, and disappear from our sight. When the ultimate object of their advancement toward perfection was achieved, behold the stars of heaven! One old he fellow, more ambitious than the rest, kept on developing until he became the sun !

And thus ends the harmonious perfection of the Darwinian theory, in a blaze of glory !

Comment is unnecessary.

E

A TALE OF THE WARS OF PONTIAC.

THE incidents of this our true story, date back over a century ago.

On the morning of the 13th of September, 1759, the flag of France waved above the ramparts of Quebec for the last time. The night previous, the army of the heroic Wolfe had scaled the fearful hights that buttressed the Plains of Abraham, and when the sun rose the astonished soldiers of Montcalm saw its rays flashing back from the bayonets of their enemies, whose compact lines were drawn up in battle array. The fierce conflict that ensued is now historical, and its events need not here be recapitulated. The treaty that followed ceded all Canada to the British crown. On the 29th of November, 1760, Detroit was surrendered to an English force.

The numerous Indian tribes of the northwest were the allies of the French, and their hatred of the English was bloody and unrelenting. Pontiac, the great chief of the fierce Ottawas, of Lake Michigan, was a savage of wonderful endowments. Eloquent and sagacious in council, fearless in battle, and with an energy that never tired or faltered, he wielded an influence over all the other tribes, never equaled by an Indian warror, until his successor, Tecumseh, appeared upon the wild scene of action.

Pontiac saw at once that the only safety of his people lay in the extermination of the encroaching English. Fired with this conviction, the fierce chief, without companionship of any kind, threaded the dark and pathless forest on a war mission to all the tribes bordering on Lakes Huron, Michigan, and Superior, and even penetrated the wilderness which held the Iroquois of the Onondaga region.   Tireless, sleepless, and inspired by a patriotic hate, that seemed to sustain him beyond natural strength, he finally succeeded in gathering a force of two thousand painted warriors, arrayed in a final effort to stay the encroachments of the white invaders.

It was in the spring of 1763, that Pontiac and his followers, accompanied by their wives and children, took the trail that led from Lake Huron to Detroit.   On his arrival he encamped a short distance from the outwork of the fort, professing a peaceful mission while anxiously awaiting the appearance of his allies.   As the different chiefs approached with their followers, they were stopped miles from the town by Pontiac, and constructed their villages beyond the reach of the knowledge of the garrison of Detroit.

In the meantime, Pontiac and his warriors, to the number of fifty, with their women and children, were permitted to enter the town at intervals to hold conferences with the English officers, and to exchange the skins of animals for trinkets, tobacco, &c.

The chief had a daughter which the French soldiers had named "Lac la Belle," or Belle of the Lake, because of her rare Indian grace and beauty.

The garrison was commanded by Capt. Gladwyn, a young English officer of great gallantry and fine personal appearance.   Lac la Belle soon came to love the English commander with all the wild fervor of her nature.   Gladwyn, in return, manifested a strong interest in the dusky maiden of the woods, and the two were in each other's company as often as brief opportunity would permit.

One day the Indian maiden entered the quarters of Gladwyn with a pair of moccasins, made by her own hands, and beautifully ornamented, which she had wrought at his request, and presented them to him. She was silent, but her face was sad and sorrowful, and her eyes suffused with tears. He questioned her as to the cause of her unwonted manner, to which she only responded with sobs. Gladwyn, supposing it to be but a momentary whim, or a loving, womanly caprice of melancholy that possessed her, tried to enliven her by a few jesting allusions to her unhappy state of feeling, when, some officers entering with reports, he led her to the door, stooped down and kissed her brow affectionately, bid her good bye, with the request that she would call again on the morrow.

Lac la Belle tottered off a few steps, sat down upon the ground, buried her face in her hands, while her long, black tresses fell forward upon her knees.

She remained in this position so long that the sentinel at the door began to think that there was something of more than common meaning in her despairing attitude and manner, and stepping inside informed his commander of the singular circumstance. Gladwyn walked to a loop-hole and observed her attentively for a few moments. He then dismissed the officers, and ordered the sentinel to bring the girl before him. The latter stepped toward her and laid his hand gently on her shoulder.

"The captain desires to speak to you," said the soldier, in a kind and compassionate tone.

Without a word, or a look of recognition to the sentinel, the girl arose to her feet and walked into the fort. Gladwyn met her at the entrance, and, taking her hand in his, led her to his private office.

"There is something unusual the matter with my forest bird to-day," he exclaimed, as he placed his arms endearingly around her neck, and kissed the tears from her eyes. "Do you think that I have ceased to love you, because at times I seem neglectful, under the over-pressing cares and anxieties of my position? The daughter of Pontiac should not grieve over childish fancies."

At the mention of her father's name a visible thrill passed through the frame of the maiden. Rising slowly to her feet, like one almost bereft of motion, she turned an agonizing look into the face of her lover, and tremulously wailed out:

"When the sun sinks down into the great water that lies beyond the mountains of the west, the white chief will take a canoe and go down the river to his brethren at Quebec? I will send one of our people with him, past the Pottawatto-mie village, on the south of the encampment, and then he will be safe. I can say no more. Will the white chief heed the words of the weak Indian girl who would die for him, but cannot save him if he remains?"

The conviction that a treacherous assault upon the place by Pontiac was matured and imminent flashed upon the mind of Gladwyn. He drew himself up to his full attitude, and a soldierly fire gleamed from his eye.

"And it is the daughter of a great chief who would counsel the one who loves her to cowardly flee from a danger he should be the first to confront? Would Lac la Belle have me to leave my comrades to the slaughter and the tor-ture of savage cruelty and seek refuge in flight? Girl, you are crazed with brooding over a terrible secret, in which my life is involved, and you know not the infamy you advise. I cannot ask you to betray your father. Go back to your people with your secret unbroken, and leave me to whatever fate craft and treachery may have prepared for myself, and the companions whose lives are entrusted to me."

Thus speaking, Gladwyn took the girl by the hand to lead her to the door. But the maiden released his clasp, and gazing into his eyes for an instant with an expression of tender and subdued pride, said :

"The white chief has spoken well, and the poor Indian girl is mad. But the Great Spirit has let a light into her heart, and there she can read what he would have her say. Listen !"

"When the sun is over the tops of the pines to-morrow, Pontiac will come into the fort with fifty chiefs, each carrying a gun that has been cut off so as to be easily hidden under their blankets. He will demand a council. At a signal every English officer will be killed, and the sentinels at the gate will be shot down by a number of our people who will be carelessly lying about on the grass at the entrance. Two hundred picked warriors will be crouched under the high banks of the river, who will then rush in, and every living white man, woman and child, is to be killed and scalped."

She paused a moment, and seemed to be painfully struggling with some internal conflict for further utterance. At last, she continued in a firmer voice, like one who has mastered her emotions :

"And now the Indian girl has told you all, and betrayed her father and her kindred to perhaps certain death. And why has she done this against those who are only trying to reclaim their own from the cruel race which has so wronged them ? She can only say it is because she loves the white chief, and can wish to die for *his* safety. She could see all his people perish, and joy in their torture. But she loves the white chief who has been so kind to her, and she cannot keep what she has revealed. The Great Spirit has spoken through the tongue of Lac la Belle."

Again she paused. But the tears were dried upon her cheek, and her whole deportment was touchingly calm and womanly. She then took a step forward, clasped the hand of the commander in both her own, laid her head upon his bosom, and said in a soft, sad voice:

"The white chief is wise, and will be prepared for to-morrow, but will shed no blood. This is all the Indian girl asks of him she loves."

So saying, she gathered her embroidered blanket about her graceful form, left the fort, passed the wondering sentinel at the gate, entered a bark canoe, and soon joined her people on the Canadian side of the river.

The morning sun rose slowly out of the eastern forest and shot his rays full upon the palisades of Detroit. The giant pines seemed transfixed in the pulseless atmosphere. All around was the sublimity of forest solitude. The garrison had been under arms all night, but as the daylight advanced into the unbroken silence, the soldiers had been dismissed for two hours of sleep. A few drowsy sentinels alone leaned motionless upon their muskets.

About ten o'clock a fleet of canoes were seen to put out from the western shore of the river toward the fort. These were filled with squaws and children, who soon swarmed into the vacant space in the rear of the wooden defenses of De-troit. An hour later Pontiac and his confederate chiefs appeared upon the ground, closely wrapped in their blankets, but all seemingly unarmed. But their dark eyes shot forth the baleful fires of anticipated massacre, as they cast furtive glances of hate upon defenses and defenders.

The chieftains reached the gate of the little town, which was at once thrown open for their admission. As the savages filed up the single street toward the council chamber, a sight met their view that startled even Pontiac from his usual stoicism, and a fierce exclamation, half strangled in its birth, escaped him. On either side of their advance stood an hundred stalwart soldiers of England, with bayoneted guns in their hands, and pistols in their belts !

Pontiac saw at a glance that his plot was either suspected or betrayed. On entering the council chamber with his followers, he sat sullenly down upon the ground, in evident doubt and perplexity. At length he arose, and with a fierce look at Gladwyn, enquired :

" Did my white brother suspect the truth of Pontiac and his people that he thus receives them as enemies ? When was the wampum of amity broken between us ? When did an Ottawa speak with forked tongue, or draw the tomahawk in a council of peace ?"

" My young men," responded Gladwyn, with a sarcastic smile, " are only receiving their warrior friends after the custom of the English. Our king would be angry with his servants if they neglected such honors when so great a chief as Pontiac was a guest under his flag."

The eye of the baffled savage gleamed like that of a rattlesnake, as he turned from the face of Gladwyn, slowly around upon the assembled officers of the fort. Once he seemed in the act of giving the signal, but on the instant the rattle of musketry without, and the deep alarm roll of the drum, dispelled what little hope he had of taking his enemy unawares. The council soon broke up without further incident, and the Indians at once departed to their own encampments on the farther side of the river.

A week had now elapsed since the events we have just narrated, and not a single savage had attempted to enter the fort, or hold parley with its defenders. Their hunting parties could be seen leaving the Ottawa village every morning, returning in the evening with canoes laden with venison, but no demonstration of either friendship or hostility broke in upon the monotony of garrison life.

But on the morning of the eighth day a canoe, in which was seated a single warrior, was seen by a sentinel to put out from the opposite shore of the river, directly toward the fort. There was a strong, skillful hand at the paddle, and on the the light craft came with a speed that excited the admiration of the half civilized hunters who made a part of the garrison, and who had crowded to the palisades the moment the sentinel had announced the coming of the canoe.

"I'll bet my rifle agin an old chaw of tobacker," exclaimed a long, gaunt, frowsy-headed trapper from the head of Lake Michigan, who had come down but the day before with a canoe load of peltries to trade at the fort, "that yonder big red devil is one of them bloody Ojibwas from Huron. There aint a Chippewa, nor a Wyandot, nor a skulking wolf of a Mingo of the Great Lake, who can put a boat through a head wind, on a straight line, like that sarpent is a doing it."

The savage had now approached near the shore, and the trapper, with hand shading his eyes, was attentively scrutinizing his appearance. Whatever the suspicions of the latter might have been when the Indian was first seen approaching, closer investigation seemed entirely to confirm them.

"May I be roasted on hemlock logs by Ottawa squaws," he suddenly broke forth, "ef that red nigger haint got a white gal's hair at his belt."

And without further words he raised his fatal rifle to his shoulder. Another second and the Indian, who had reached the shore, and was about pulling his boat up on the sandy slope, would have received a leaden passport to the happy hunting ground. But just then a strong arm seized the trapper by his long matted locks, and hurled him backward upon the ground. His rifle was discharged as he was falling, and the contents passed harmlessly into the air. It was Gladwyn who had thus opportunely arrived, and saved the life of the intended victim.

"Take that chattering idiot to the fort," he exclaimed, "and chain him to a picket until we can deal with him as his offense demands. Such fools are the cause of nearly all the blood that is spilled in these wars, and must be taught the rules of Christian warfare."

The discomfited trapper was led off by a file of soldiers, but as he went he turned his face to Gladwyn and said:

"Cap'in, mayhap you'll see afore you're much older that Ingins will be Ingins, and your 'Christian warfare' aint 'zackly the medicine to cure their complaint. When you've lived in these here woods as long as I have, and larned more of the ways of the red varmints, p'raps you'll git your eye teeth cut, and p'raps you won't. At any rate, I know I'm right, and will try the same thing over agin on the first durn'd redskin that comes within reach of my rifle, wearing a white gal's scalp. So, Cap'in, ef that aint your style, you mout as well shoot me right here."

In the meantime the Indian, who was evidently unarmed, had pushed his boat hastily back into the water on the report of the rifle, and then turned to reconnoitre. Apparently satisfied that the demonstration was not intended for him, he again beached his canoe, and wrapping his blanket around him so as to hide the hideous trophy that had so enraged the trapper, strode up to the gate of the fort.

He was admitted by the commander in person, and at once proceeded to announce his mission.

"Pontiac wants the Englishman, with as many of his young men as he chooses to bring with him, to come over at once to the Ottawa village to a council."

"And why," rejoined Gladwyn, "does my brother make

such a request now for the first time ? He has always heretofore came with his warriors to the fort, when he wished a
talk with his English friends. Has he not been suffered to
depart in peace as he came, and with many presents from his
white father, the King ?"

"Pontiac is a mighty chief, and his braves are of many
tribes, and as numerous as the pigeons that come from the
south when the leaves are reddened by the frost and the beach
nuts fall to the ground. The messenger has but to deliver
his words, and has no right to know their meaning. When
the sun begins to turn the shadows of the hemlocks toward
the north, Wawatam will return to him who sent him."

So saying the huge savage sat down upon the ground, lit
his pipe, and refused all further conversation. Nor would he
partake of the hospitality freely tendered him by officers and
soldiers. He continued to smoke in calm indifference to his
surroundings, and never once returned the look of the curious
idlers who had gathered around him. He wore the elk skin
moccasin of the Ojibwas, the fiercest and bloodiest of all the
savages of the Great Lakes.

The trapper before mentioned was fastened with a dog
chain to a post within the fort, but the door was open so that
he could look out upon the scene in front. The bearer of
Pontiac's message sat about fifty yards distant, and upon him
the prisoner stared with a look of perplexed uncertainty. At
last he said to the sentinel :

"See here, red coat, just send one of your fellers over to
that Ingin, and see if the little finger of his left hand aint
mis'in."

The soldier was a kindly, good-natured man, and at once
requested a comrade to stroll over and carelessly make the
desired investigation. The result confirmed what the trapper
had suggested. With a stifled burst of rage he muttered :

"The Ojibwa thief and murderer! He has the hair of my brother and his little boy, in his wigwam by the outlet of the Upper Huron! And here am I, chained like a dog to his kennel! Damn that 'Christian warfare' of an English Captain! A smooth-faced boy to teach old Joe Lukens what's manners among redskins!"

He shook his head a few moments in silence, and then resumed in a low voice, as if arguing against a resolve that he could hardly reconcile to his conscience.

"No, no; the meddling youngster only did his duty, I suppose, accordin' to his light. He came from a country over the seas, where the Quebec traders say there is nothin' but cities, and ignorant people who live in houses, and where half the men, women and children starve, that a few of their breatheren may, accordin' to missionary talk up to Michillimackinac, dress in purple and fine linen, and fare sumtooisly every day."

Again he paused. Again shook his head deprecatingly. Again continued:

"I can't bring myself to hate that boy of an English captain, and to act accordingly when I git clear of this infarnal hole, where a woodman can scace git his breath. There was a day, when I first went out with the French of Montreal agin the cussed Iroquois of the Six Nations, when I would a twisted his neck off for sich as this, with as little compunction as I would that of a wounded patridge. But I was young then, and I fear, as bloody minded as a wild Mingo, when the war-whoop sounded in the woods by Lake Ontary. But I 'spose the English lad only did his duty acordin' to his light, and that is the most the best of us kin do, acordin' to the missionary doctern."

"But," he shouted, after a short pause, and springing to the length of his iron tether, "does the brat, in his braided soldier fixins, think this chain can hold me longer than I choose to be dog-tied to his pine stick ?"

The sentinel here lowered his bayonet to the breast of the prisoner, and commanded silence. The trapper smiled, and sat down upon a low bench.

"Fergive me, comrade," he exclaimed, "I aint got nothin' agin you, you are only doin' acordin' to your bringin' up, and you would be shot acordin' to 'Christian warfare,' as the boy has it, if you showed you was a white man of the woods, and let me out of this badger's den. Your ways aint as my ways, and I aint got anything agin you. But before the moon lights up the eastern forest, Joe Lukens will be either a dead lump of earth, or a free man of the wilderness. He would rather take his chances with the Ingins, than be chained with the white men of 'Christian warfare !'"

As we have said before, Gladwyn was a brave and fearless soldier. He had his doubts about the intentions of the savages in thus demanding his presence in their midst, but rather than show doubt and timidity, he resolved to brave the consequences. As the hour indicated by the Ojibwa messenger approached, he selected three of his trustiest subordinates, and informed the savage that he was ready to go with him.

The Indian arose without a word, led the way out of the gate, down to the river, and the party entered the boat. A few minutes brought them to the other side, where Pontiac, and fully a hundred painted chiefs and warriors stood ready to receive them.

No greetings passed between the parties as they met, and a sullen hostility marked the expression in the face of each warrior. Even the squaws and children, who usually manifest delight at the gathering of a peaceful council between

their people and the whites, now wore a look hungry for
blood.

Pontiac pointed to a log enclosure, covered with hemlock
branches, and led the way. The line filed in and formed a
circle, placing the Englishmen in the centre. Every action
thus far had a look ominous of danger. A hundred, deep
set, black, snaky eyes, shed a lurid light of hate upon the
four unarmed men, but not a sound had yet been uttered.

Pontiac raised his right hand, and his warriors at once
squatted upon the ground. He then took one step forward
from the circle, and looking for a moment steadily into the
eyes of Gladwyn, whose face was paler than usual, but firm
of expression, spoke as follows :

"The Chief of the Ottawas has but few words for the ear
of the servant of the English King. But these shall be the
words of truth. The tongue that, says one thing while the
heart means another has been heard between us until we are
ashamed of ourselves, and our eyes wander from the faces we
are trying to deceive. Two thousand warriors are in the
woods within sight of the smoke of Detroit. They have
come to push the English from the place they have stolen.
Deliver up the fort, go back to your own people, and the
word of Pontiac will keep you and your young men from
harm on the way. What has my brother to say?"

Gladwyn stood silent a few moments, as one who is trying
to reflect upon the bearing of an unexpected proposition.
Then, in a low and distinct voice, and a calm and determined
manner, he said :

"The great chief of the Ottawas is angry, and knows not
what he asks. A bad spirit has got between my brother and
the light, and would lead his people to destruction. They
sold this land to the French, and received the price. The
French King went to war with the English and was con-

quered. A great council was held, and a treaty of peace made, in which all this country claimed by the French, and held by them, was yielded up to my people, and—"

Here Pontiac, whose impatient rage at the claims of Gladwyn had given him the look of a demon during these brief words, threw his blanket from his shoulders, and with a majesty of mien that seemed of inspiration, strode close in front of his adversary, and with arm outstretched toward heaven, and eye turned upon his followers, exclaimed :

" The tongue of the Englishman is the tongue of a liar, and should be torn out by the roots. There never was a time, since the Great Spirit made the world, and gave this heritage to his red children, in which our fathers have not been in the possession of the country, its woods, its lakes, and the great plains on which no trees grow. The Frenchman came, not many moons since, and the red man gave him lands on which to hunt, and waters in which to fish. They were his only at the will of our people. We had more than we needed, and the Great Manito of the red man told us to receive the white strangers as our brothers. The French King came, not with guns to command, but with tongue to request. The chain of friendship was held by a red hand at the north, and a white hand at the south. There was blood upon neither, and all the links were brightened in the rays of peace. The Englishman came, like a wolf among deer, and stirred up strife between us. He lied to our young men, and they went on the war path against their friends at Quebec. Then at last, the cunning Englishman came in and laid claim upon all the country, while its true owners were weakened like children, with the loss of blood."

Then turning full upon Gladwyn, the aroused savage rather yelled than spoke :

" Yes, liar, with the double tongue, you came here as

wanderers and beggars, and now you would remain as con-
querors and owners!"

Then wheeling slowly around upon the circle of his warriors, he continued:

"And now what is to be done with these *prisoners?*"

In an instant each warrior leaped to his feet, a glittering
knife gleamed in each hand, held far above the head, while
the startled echoes of the forest responded from its depths to
yells, such as no human ear ever heard from human throats,
other than those of North American savages when aroused to
a carnival of blood.

The treacherous chief gazed a few moments proudly upon
his ferocious followers, who intently watched his every motion, expectant of the signal that was to let loose their fury
upon the pale but unflinching prisoners. He raised his
hand, and every Indian replaced his scalping-knife, and sank
slowly down upon the ground.

"An Ottawa never sheds blood in his council lodge, unless
his enemies are equal in numbers. The English captain
will remain. His young men can go."

In an instant the savages gathered around the three officers
who had accompanied their commander, and hurried them
out of the lodge. They had scarcely disappeared, leaving
Pontiac and Gladwyn alone, when

> "At once there rose so wild a yell,
>   As if all the fiends from Heaven that fell,
>   Had pealed the battle cry of hell!"

The shrill screams of the squaws and children, mingled with
the hoarse howls of the warriors, and the low groans of
mortal agony that filled the lull in the yells of the demons,
told but too plainly, to the wretched English captain, the
fate of his companions.

In a few moments a gigantic savage, with face smeared with blood and brains, entered the lodge. It was Wawatam, the Ojibwa envoy of the morning. Without a word, he approached Pontiac, and throwing down a matted and bloody mass at the feet of the chief, departed as silently as he had approached.

Maddened beyond all bounds of moral restraint at the sight of the bleeding scalps of his faithful comrades of fort and field, Gladwyn turned to the Ottawa chief, with dauntless and defiant mien, and in measured and unfaltering tones, said :

"The blood of the slain—murdered treacherously in a council of peace—be upon the head of Pontiac and his people. Henceforth I will hunt his warriors, his squaws, and his children, as wolves and their cubs are hunted, without mercy. On the waters, in the wilderness, wherever an Ottawa or his allies paddles a canoe or erects a lodge, will the bullets of the English seek victims, until none are left for the chase or the war path. I swear this before the murderer of my comrades!"

Ere these words had hardly left the tongue that uttered them, Pontiac sprang with a bound in front of the Englishman, with tomahawk uplifted above his head. The face of the savage was distorted with a hellish rage, such as no painter ever drew, or no sculptor ever wrought! The captive quailed not for an instant, but met the demoniac gaze of the warrior, with an eye as fearless, if not as baleful, as his own.

The two thus confronted each other for the space of a minute, and the Indian slowly lowered his weapon, and returned it to his girdle. The intensity of his ferocious look was relaxed, but its unrelenting determination was still there, as he exclaimed:

"The white warrior is brave, but he has no strength, and his words are the words of a woman. There are many trees between Detroit and the great lakes, with a warrior of my people behind each. The English captain forgets himself. He will go no more upon the war path. When the sun lifts the darkness from the river in the morning, so that the eyes of my people can know what their hands do, the white chief dies. The squaws and children of Pontiac are now gathering the wood that will consume him in its fires. My people will see if a warrior of the English King can boast so bravely in the flames as in the council chamber."

The chief paused, and uttered a low guttural sound. Instantly two savages entered and approached Gladwyn, and led him to a stake firmly driven in the ground, by one corner ot the lodge. They then proceeded to tie his hands and feet securely to the post, with thongs of deer skin, in such a manner that he was forced to stand upright, without the power to change, in the least, his position. This accomplished, Pontiac and the two Indians departed, leaving the victim alone.

Slowly the sun sank down behind the deep, dark forests of the western horizon, and the twilight came on, and thickened into night. The silent stars came forth one by one, and took up their appointed places in the vault of eternity. The giant trees bent their tops toward each other, as the wind wrestled with their foliage, and whispered of the centuries that had fled since they were saplings in the soil.

The young English soldier was still alone, in the painful bonds of his captors. But the agony of thought deadened his physical sufferings. He knew that Pontiac was the bloodiest and most unrelenting of his fierce race, and that his many great wrongs had driven him into a mood of ferocious insanity. He had never yet betrayed the confidence reposed in him by the French, but from the English his people had only received outrage and injustice. He revenged himself according to his Indian nature, which was tireless in pursuit, and merciless in execution.

The young soldier was a bound captive in the wilderness of the New World, and the silent shadow of Death was creeping in upon him. But his thoughts were not of himself. They were wandering over the broad expanse of forest and river, of mountain and prairie, over across three thousand miles of watery waste to the little cot on the banks of the Severn, that held all most dear to him of earth—his widowed mother, his only sister. It was hard to die thus, so young, so strong, so wedded to life by all the ties that make the most courageous natures shrink from the dread silence of the grave. Anon the current of his thoughts returned to his present surroundings, and the sad face of the daughter of Pontiac looked up out of his vision. Was she safe? Had she escaped the detection and the vengeance of her father?

The big tears welled up into the eyes of the young soldier, and dropped, " pat," " pat," " pat," upon the dry leaves amid which he stood. When hope has deserted one in the hour of dire extremity, memory softens the hardest heart into the weakness of a child.

A slight noise outside now came to the acute ear of the captive, and on the instant two stalwart Indians entered. One was Wawatam, the Ojibwa, and the other a favorite young chief of Pontiac. Each was armed with gun, pistols, and scalping knife. They advanced toward Gladwyn and closely examined his bonds. Satisfied with the scrutiny, the young savage sat down upon the ground within · a few feet of the prisoner, while the Ojibwa went outside and took up a position at the door. Not a word had been spoken.

Slowly the hours waned on. Midnight had approached, and all sounds had ceased in the Indian encampment.

In an hour thereafter, a form dimly seen in the darkness,

slowly, and without the least sound from the yielding sand, snaking its way along toward a clump of bushes that stood at one corner of the chamber, and between the sentinel and the approaching object. Whatever the mysterious creature was, man or animal, it evidently meant mischief. When the back of the Indian was turned, the stealthy object would make a rapid advance, and when the former again faced the river, the latter would lay prone among the surrounding logs, from which it could not be distinguished. At last the clump of bushes was reached, and the creature lay still within the cover.

In about fifteen minutes more, a light form, closely wrapped in a blanket, advanced out of the darkness into the dim light of the fire that smouldered near the spot where the sentinel now squatted upon the sand. The savage started to his feet, leveled his gun, and uttered a low sound. A whispered response, and the chief lowered his weapon, resumed his seat, and the form passed into the council chamber. The young warrior within uttered an ejaculation of surprise.

Gladwyn looked up. *Lac la Belle stood before him!*

An expression of joy lit up the pale features of the Englishman, as he recognized the maiden, which was about to express itself in words, when with a quick and intelligent gesture, she imposed silence. Then she approached the sentinel, took his hand, looked up in his face with a beseeching smile, and said:

"Miantanoba, listen. You have told me that you loved the daughter of Pontiac. Release the English captain, and she promises to fly with you wherever you may direct, and be the wife of your wigwam. Lac la Belle swears this, and the Great Spirit hears her."

Wawatam, without, had his ear to a crevice between the logs, and was listening intently.

The young chief within replied to the Indian maiden:

"Lac la Belle loves the Englishman, and it is for his sake that she will become the wife of Miantanoba. The dog shall die."

"The white chief has been kind to the Indian girl," replied the maiden, "and she would save him. This is all she can say. The time is short. Will Miantanoba listen to my words?"

Wawatam pressed his ear closer to the aperture, and his face was distorted with a horrible ferocity.

"The dog shall die," repeated the young Indian, "and Lac la Belle will be the wife of Miantanoba, or Pontiac shall know that she loves the Englishman, and betrayed her people."

The Indian turned away from the suppliant. Quick as lightning she drew a long knife from the folds of her blanket, and struck its glittering blade deep into the heart of the savage. He reeled a moment, clutched at his tomahawk, and fell dead.

A loud yell from the Ojibwa startled the sleeping echoes of the surrounding forests to their depths for miles. But ere that wild cry could be repeated, a dark object leaped up from the ground, seized the gigantic warrior by his long scalp lock, bent his head back, and drew a sharp knife across his throat, nearly severing the head from the body.

"Blast yer durned red hide, stop that hollerin'!" exclaimed the trapper, as the huge savage lay squirming and gasping at his feet.

With a single bound the trapper cleared the dying form of his enemy and stood within the enclosure. Lac la Belle had already cut the thongs that had |bound her lover, but his benumbed limbs refused the efforts of his will, and the captive had sank to the ground. In an instant the trapper seized the

prostrate form and swung it to his shoulder, as though it had
but the weight of an infant.

"Gal, quick, lead the way to the river," he whispered, and
the two were soon in rapid flight in that direction.

Scarce a minute had elapsed from the war whoop of the
Ojibwa, to the release of the Englishman, and yet th ewhole
encampment was alarmed, and wild yells and hurrying feet
could be heard through the darkness. Pontiac was the first
to hear the death cry of the sentinel, and leaping from
his couch, sought to grasp his gun. But it was gone! He
shouted for his daughter. She was not there! The chief
gave a prolonged yell of rage, grasped his bow and a
sheaf of arrows that lay in a corner of the lodge, and rushed
out toward the council chamber.

The Indians had evidently mistaken the cause of this night
alarm. They naturally supposed that a rescuing party from
the fort had been discovered by the sentinels, and were running in every direction, the darkness adding to their confusion.

Pontiac, followed by a few chiefs, entered the council chamber. The dead body of the sentinel, and the blanket of Lac
la Belle close by the stake to which the Englishman had been
bound, told the story.

As the truth flooded fully upon the understanding of the
fierce savage, the agony depicted upon his distorted features
was fearful to look upon. He seemed like a demon paralyzed
with rage. His breast heaved, and sobs and groanings issued
therefrom. He clutched his throat, like one strangling with
his emotions. The hated enemy of his race escaped, and his
daughter the betrayer of her people! All his plans, all his
hopes thwarted in a moment.

This scene lasted but a few seconds. A succession of loud
yells, followed by the discharge of several guns in the direction of the canoes, awakened the chief from his delirium of

rage and despair. With the leap of a deer he cleared the threshold of the cabin, and sped away toward the river. Hundreds of his warriors had here gathered, and were running up and down like infuriated madmen. Dimly seen in the far darkness of the river were the outlines of a single canoe, from which came the occasional splash of a paddle. All the rest of the fleet had been cut adrift long before the alarm, for none but the one that was propelled toward the opposite shore was in sight!

But the quick eye of Pontiac soon discovered a boat about fifty yards distant, which had been caught in the eddy of a rock. Without a word he plunged into the water, his weapon at his back. A few moments sufficed to place the desperate chief in possession of the canoe, and the chase began.

The foremost boat had now got beyond the dark shadows which the tall forest had thrown upon the waters. In its prow could be seen the daughter of Pontiac, with the head of Gladwyn resting upon her knees. In the stern sat the trapper, with skilled hand at the paddle.

The old man was chuckling all over with suppressed glee, at an adventure he had evidently commenced relating to ears that heard not, for he continued:

" Yes, cap'in, its a mighty handy thing to have a file somewhere about your clothes, when you happen to drift among people who keep dog chains for white men, and then go off alone to palaver with red Injins. Not that I blame you for goin' acordin' to your bringin' up. Some folks never larn anything, ony what they got to home. Sich hev no bisness in the woods, specially when Injins are about. Cap'in, what's your 'pinion of 'Christian warfare,' jist about this time? Thet skelp of yourn aint jist safe yet, but you will hev time to give your 'pinion upon 'Christian warfare' before that red devil off yonder ketches up with us."

The trapper here paused again to indulge in another chuckle, which he seemed to enjoy amazingly.

" Well, Cap'in," he resumed, "that sentinel of yourn went off into a doze like, and then I begun to snore like a drunken Frenchman. Bimeby he snored too, natural like. I had spiled your dog chain afore dark, while that chap had gone to git his rashuns. And so, when I knowed there warn't no make b'lieve about that snore of his'n, I jist snapped the durn'd link close to my ankle, jumped squar over his head, knocked down the feller outside the door, and went over the stockade like an Injin thief in the night, swum the river, and you and your gal knows the rest. Cap'in, you won't be mean enough to chain a feller up agin for this, on ' Christian warfare ' rules, if I git you and the gal back agin, safe to the fort, will you?"

The trapper fairly laughed outright at the conclusion of his remarks, for the humor of the thing seemed so irresistible. So absorbed had he become in the recital of his escape from the fort, and in avenging his wrongs in quiet sarcasm at the author of them, that he had began to relax his efforts at the paddle, and had, in a manner, withdrawn his attention from the pursuit. All of a sudden the deep clouds over head parted, and the full moon came forth and illumined the entire bed of the river. The trapper looked hurriedly around. The canoe of Pontiac was less than thirty yards in the rear. The trapper now made a desperate effort to increase the distance, when the paddle snapped short off in his hands!

"Curse my babbling tongue," he exclaimed, and his whole nature seemed to change at once. He answered the triumphant yell which Pontiac had uttered on being discovered, by a shout of defiance which echoed over the waters, and was even sent back from the defences of the fort, now plainly visible in the moonlight.

" Am I a fool from the great cities, that I prattle like a boy, when I should be silent and watchful over the lives that are in my keeping," he yelled, starting to his feet, and looking around vainly for a weapon.

" Not even a knife," he bitterly muttered, " and a helpless man, and a feeble girl to be murdered before my eyes, unless I am killed first, which I pray God may happen."

He was interrupted by a scream from the Indian girl, as she sprang up, and threw herself in front of the young Englishman. At the same instant an arrow whizzed past the trapper, and found lodgment in the breast of Lac la Belle.

Pontiac stood in the prow of his canoe, his splendid form clearly revealed in the moonlight, gazing intently ahead in an effort to ascertain the effect of his shot.

" It is well," he murmured, in a sad tone. " The arrow was aimed at another, but the Great Spirit directed its flight to the heart of her who would die for one of the accursed race. The daughter of Pontiac will soon be no more, but the Englishman, for whom she betrayed her people, shall go with her."

The savage deliberately placed another arrow to his bow, but ere he could draw the string, the sound of cannon rang from the fort, a number of balls splashed the water close to the boats, the canoe of Pontiac was knocked to pieces, and left the chief struggling in the water. At the same instant a boat filled with soldiers came in full view, and with a few more strokes of the oar was along side of the one that contained the fugitives.

A few seconds sufficed for a hurried explanation, the canoe was fastened to the boat of the rescuing party, which had, by this time, turned its prow toward the fort. Neither Gladwyn nor the trapper was aware that the fatal arrow of Pontiac had found lodgment in the bosom of his daughter. She sat with her face bent downward upon her knees, and paid no attention to what was going on around her.

As the boat rounded for the shore, the trapper leaned over to one of the soldiers and whispered:

"Red coat, jist, accidentally like, hand me that smooth-bore of yourn. There is a murderin' redskin a paddlin' around out yonder, that wants a leetle help in his diffikilty. It is a shame to see a feller creter drown, when an ounce of lead could save him."

The Indian maiden raised her head quickly, and said:

"The white hunter may have a daughter among his own people. He will spare the life of the father of Lac la Belle?"

At the sound of her voice, Gladwyn aroused himself from his stupor and putting his hand upon the arm of the trapper, said, in his old tone of command:

"Man, you have saved my life, and what there is in my power to bestow upon you is for you to ask, or accept. But if you take the life of the chief, you shall die on the instant."

"Well!" said the trapper, with a look of indignant amazement, "what next? This goslin-hearted boy would hvae been roasted alive before noon to day, and the red devil who would hev lit the fire, is still within reach of a good aim, and not one of these fellers dare hand me a gun! A little more of this 'Christian warfare,' and there won't be a white scalp left on its owner's head, between Detroit and Huron. It's about time that Joe Lukens went back to the settlements, and joined the Methodists, or put on a petticoat and hired hisself out to nuss young niggers on the Virginia plantations!"

Thus muttering, the trapper seated himself, with a look of inexpressible disgust, but his feelings were too powerful for continued silence.

"I can't say I blame the gal. The bloody heathen was her father, and wimming nater' is the same, in the woods, or

in the cities. I couldn't hev killed the cuss, arter she spoke
so pleading like, onless he'd a hed his infernal knife at my
own throat. But as for that brat of an English cap'in,"—

The grating of the boat upon the gravelly shore, and the
immediate preparations for landing, cut short the unfinished
growlings of the angry trapper. A dozen soldiers, with pine
torches in their hands, and anxious inquiry in their faces, stood
ready to receive their comrades. At the sight of their commander and his two companions, the main facts of the case
were at once comprehended, and cheer after cheer rent the
general silence. These were taken up by a hundred throats
within the fort, and in defiance of all discipline and danger,
the whole garrison—men, women, and children, rushed fran-
tically down to the landing.

By this time Gladwyn had nearly recovered from his dazed
bewilderment, and began to issue his orders with something
of his old soldierly spirit. He released the hand of the Indian maiden, which up to this time he had held closely in his
own, though neither had spoken to the other from the commencement of the fearful adventure to its close, and with the
assistance of a soldier, stepped upon the shore. He turned
and addressed Lac la Belle in a soft and tender voice :

"The preserver of my life will arise and come into the fort,
where I can thank her devoted heroism and loving regard, as
I cannot do here."

The girl stirred not, and made no sign. But in the
now hushed silence, her stifled breathing, and low choking
sobs, could be distinctly heard. The soldiers, who had
crowded round, looked wonderingly into each other's faces for
explanation of the sad and touching behavior of the maiden.

A loud exclamation—almost a shriek—fell from the lips of
the trapper, who, since the boat touched, had sat in sullen
silence upon the bottom of the canoe.

"The arrow—the gal is dying!" he gasped out, and, springing to his feet, he lifted her up gently in his arms, stepped ashore, and strode rapidly through the parted crowd toward the fort.

Gladwyn caught the exclamation, and knew at once its dread import. He stood a moment like one from whom life had suddenly departed, uttered a suppressed moan, and then, assisted by a soldier on either side, tottered on in the direction of the others.

Lac la Belle lay upon a bed, the rude trapper kneeling beside her, sobbing like an infant. The surgeon was in attendance, and had extracted the arrow, just as Gladwyn staggered into the room. He motioned for the soldiers who had crowded around, to leave. Then there were none by the bedside of the dying girl, save the commander, the surgeon, and the trapper.

"There is no hope," whispered the surgeon, in answer to an imploring look from the young officer.

Gladwyn approached the bed, bent over the silent sufferer, and pressed his lips fondly to hers. The maiden slowly opened her eyes, a tender, loving smile illuminated her face. She feebly raised her arms, entwined them about the neck of her lover, and drew his face down upon her bosom. A few moments thus passed in silence, when the surgeon stepped forward, and softly released the clasp of the girl.

"This will not do," he whispered into the ear of Gladwyn. "Her time is but brief, and she may have something important to say before she departs."

Gladwyn raised himself to his feet. His vest was clotted with blood—the blood of the dying.

At this moment a Jesuit missionary, who had just arrived at the fort, glided into the room.

The trapper still knelt as at first, but gave no sign. Not a sound escaped him.

Gladwyn again bent over the maiden, and in a whisper choked by emotion, asked her if she had any request to make.

The question seemed instantly to revive her. In a low voice she said:

"It may be a wild and foolish wish. I know that my spirit is passing away, or I would not say the words. Will the white chief make the daughter of Pontiac his wife, after the custom of his own people?"

Instantly Gladwyn knelt down, took the girl's hand in his own, and motioned to the priest.

And there in the hour and article of death, these two beings were pledged to each other in marriage, and the missionary pronounced a benediction upon their union.

Then the soldier arose to his feet, softly lifted the head of his wife from the pillow, and laid his cheek against hers. She threw her arms about his neck, and with a look of ineffable happiness whispered:

"*Husband!*"

Her head fell back. Gladwyn looked into her face and uttered a low cry.

Lac la Belle had died in his arms.

MY FIRST HUNT IN MY NEW HOME.

I HAD congratulated myself that the "Old Settler" did not deceive a credulous emigrant when he assured me that the weather here in Northern Michigan, owing to the mild influence of the lake, was of about the same temperature in winter as in New Jersey. In great peace of mind I rested in this delusion until that great day of the heart, Christmas, came, with its simple blessings and enjoyments to the lonely and neglected children of our wilderness world. But on the evening of that day the scales fell from my eyes, and icicles took their places. An unusual roaring of the great lake, and a prolonged irregular moaning of the winds, heralded the gathering elemental agitation. The North Pole was evidently stirring up the animals. And now a continuous roar in the forest told me that Boreas had stripped himself to an extra effort. His icy breath gathered fresh volume with each inhalation. The snow came down in blinding sheets of drift, which were caught up by the angry gale, and hurled back to the clouds from whence they had been cast forth. Fantastic shapes and wierd devices were in the instant designed and sculptured upon my cabin window

"By the elfin fingers of the Frost."

In brief, it came on the coldest night I ever experienced, and how I survived to give it this historic record puzzles my yet unthawed understanding.

But the "Old Settler," with the proverbial honesty of his race, assures me that in the fifteen years he has lived on the Lake Shore, he never knew as cold a winter as the present. Doubtless he asseverated the same thing to my predecessor last year this time, and will continue to unwind the same yarn to the next newcomer, unless, as I fervently hope, he may be suddenly cut off and that without remedy.

" But what has all this wordy, windy, inappropo introductory to do with the subject matter suggested by your heading?"

It is a provoked inquiry, O justifiable interrupter, and shall be truly and unreservedly answered :

Nothing! only nothing, and nothing more. But it was packed atop my mental hamper, and had to be unloaded ere the true matter could be reached.

And thus, like a camel re-assured by the removal of a harrassing burden, I proceed with renewed pace through the desert of my destination. I will now give you a faithful compilation of my first hunting expedition in these gorgeous wilds.

From childhood I was a mighty hunter—in imagination. Western border adventure constituted my chief reading, and Leather Stocking was my ideal of a hero and a man. But in New Jersey, the land of my birth and boyhood, there was no game in the animal line of greater calibre than the ferocious rabbit, and in the feathered way the robin stood, or rather flew, pre-eminent. Living all my life in cities, I seldom had opportunity to practice my cruel designs even upon these.

But when in an evil hour Satan, through his innocent agent, Horace Greeley, called upon me to " go west," visions of bear, deer, wild turkeys, and other beasts and birds, each after his kind, danced through my enkindled imagination, and I started forth with a whole arsenal of destructive arms.

First was a new English double barrel breech loader, of laminated steel, for which I paid $100, (per ninety days note of hand, which the fortunate seller still holds among his assets as a panic bankrupt, good of itself, as Jay Gould's Northern Pacifics, but difficult of realization until congress inflates the currency sufficiently to tide over many things now apparently grounded beyond hope, or the reach of resurrection. This is a rather long parenthesis, but truth is mighty and will prevail.) This was supplemented (not the parenthesis, but the gun mentioned above,) by a single barrel of assured excellence. Then came a Springfield musket, which I had patriotically carried (by a $600 substitute,) all through the war of the rebellion. A short and beautiful Wesson rifle, and a Spencer seven shooter army carbine, completed the armament with which I started for my new home in the Northwest. Of course I expected to find deer innumerable, in the woods immediately surrounding my little "clearing," and to be chased by a bear every time I went down to the log barn to feed "Fritz," my diminutive but vicious scrub of a Canadian pony.

Filled with content and happiness at the novelty of my new life, I shouldered my Wesson, a few days after my arrival, and struck out into the solemn primeval forest. My destination was Au Sable Lake, three miles distant, and the way was pointed out to me by a Norwegian neighbor, he being one of the three only settlers of our locality.

The scene as I entered the dark wilderness, was so different from all my past associations, that I soon became absorbed in reflections, solemn and suggestive. The dense and silent solitude was filled with huge trees, whose first roots had struck into the soil centuries before Columbus bored the slothful rulers of Genoa and Spain, with his vagaries of a New World. Mighty hemlocks were here, whose trunks, near the ground, measured five feet in diameter, and whose individual years numbered five centuries. Hundreds of such lay prone amid these solitudes, the victims of fire, of age, and of decay, and it requires a strong and active hunter to thread his way amid these barriers to progress. The scene to me presented the fanciful idea, that in some age long past, there had been a battle of the forests, and the slain had been left to blanch and moulder where they had fallen !

In about an hour I reached Au Sable, and found it a lovely sheet of water, about three miles in circumference, of crystal clearness, and belted with pine trees, whose green tops were proof against the season's changes, and which suggest thoughts of the glorious summer time, even when the winter rages in unrestrained fury.

But what sent the blood tingling from citadel to extremities, and gave uncontrollable nervousness to body and limbs, was the long lines of geese and ducks that were feeding in the distance upon the serge and celery of the shallow places in the lake. I felt that my hour of success as a hunter had arrived, and that my next letters to expectant friends at the East would shine with the resplendent record of my exploits.

I got down upon my hands and knees and crawled the third of a mile to a clump of bushes that stood between me and my intended victims. The journey proved a laborious and exhausting one to a rather fleshy man, whose running weight is one hundred and eighty pounds. But expectation sustained me, and I reached the coveted ambush at last. With a heart that beat time to my excitement, and seemed determined to break out and see the "sport,".I cautiously raised my head above the low sand. ridge. Nimrod & Co., what a sight ! At least ten thousand wild fowl were in view! ·But the nearest line was all of one hundred and fifty yards from my cover. 1 lay prone for a full half hour, shaking all over with novel excitement, waiting for a nearer approach of the game. At the end of this time my movements had evidently been discovered. The enemy broke up his regular formations, and gathered in little squads to discuss the situation. They bobbed their heads up and down suspiciously, sailed here and there in narrow circles, and seemed to keep up a knowing conversation as to the proper mode of procedure. At last one old fellow, a sort of admiral Drake of the fleet, whose green head glistened gorgeously in the sunlight, swam out toward me, first presenting one side and then the other, and finally came to a full halt at a distance of about fifty yards from my hiding place.

My nervousness had now fearfully increased. I shook all over, like one with the double-breasted ague. Finally I managed to rest my rifle upon a dead limb, and tried to take aim. But my vision seemed to blur every object. In vain I tried to bring the muzzle of my piece upon the intended victim. There seemed to be four barrels to my rifle, while about fourteen "sights" waltzed up and down, backward and forward, and all around the end thereof!

At last I managed to pull trigger at a wild and desperate venture. A sharp crack, and then I looked out anxiously for the effect. The old drake raised himself up on his hind legs, gave his wings a few flaps and settled down again quietly in the same spot. After two or three minutes of effort I managed to get another cartridge into the "death-dealing" weapon. With increased trepidation I sent another bullet after that invulnerable, imperturbable green-headed monster! He acknowledged the compliment precisely as at first! I fired two more shots in quick succession, with the same pantomime as the afterpiece from the party of the first part! Finding that the cuss was inclined to be facetious at my expense, I retired from the scene in disgust, and plunged

into the forest followed by a most awful din of "quack,"
"quack," "quack!" from the whole company!

Just as the gloom and silence of the woods began to deepen
around me, and while absorbed in meditation over the obdu-
racy of Michigan ducks, a fearful screech issued from a lofty
hemlock, right over my head! In an instant I felt bodily
petrified to the spot, but with every mental faculty sharpened
to an intensity never felt before. All that my youthful days
had ever heard or read about panthers, came flashing back
upon memory. I remembered how the treacherous varmints
would lay crouched upon huge limbs, and as the weary trav-
eler passed under, a scream, followed by an instantaneous
spring, heralded his doom! The hair of my head stood up,
like that of the chap who saw the vision in Job. The rifle
dropped from my nerveless grasp! The "mighty hunter"
was as helpless as a child in the presence of this sudden and
unseen danger! Romance had fled at the first approach of
reality.

The seconds thus passed seemed like hours in duration.
Slowly my numbed physical faculties recalled themselves to
partial activity. I raised my eyes to the fascinating point of
danger, just as the horrible sound was repeated!

And there was the forest-fiend in full view! It was the
limb of a tall pine tree, the body of which had blown over
against an adjacent hemlock, and as the wind swayed the support, the friction of the infernal limb gave forth the sound
that had so paralyzed my faculties!

The discovery brought instantaneous relief; and with an
attempt at a smile, which was not as successful as one interested could have wished, I picked up my rifle and resumed
the hunt.

About a mile further on I passed the cabin of a wood
chopper; and leading directly from a little outlying shed I

discovered, in the light snow which still remained in the woods, the fresh track of a deer! It was of unusually large size, and I set it down as having been made by an immense buck. Having but a vague, city idea of the animal and his appetites and habits, I surmised that the prowler had been depredating upon the poor man's henroost, and in this thought sought justification in an attempt to slay him, although the law then protected such game as "out of season."

And so I pursued the track with all the excitement of a novice in the hunting business, anxious to bring down an illustrious antlered denizen of the wilds. At intervals all along the trail I could see where the animal had rooted the snow away, that he might reach the food beneath, and these signs at last became so fresh that I knew a few minutes more must bring on the crisis. All of a sudden I saw a movement in the thick undergrowth a short distance ahead! This discovery brought on the "buck ager," as the natives denominate that shaking attack which always seizes upon the hunter when called to confront his first deer, still I pushed cautiously forward, my heart sounding like the rapid thumping of shore water under a beached canoe.

All at once I saw that the track had left the old lumber trail, and turned to the left into the woods. I stopped a moment to reconnoitre. Suddenly with a loud succession of grunts, the enemy leaped from behind a huge hemlock into the middle of the road, and drew up in crescent-shaped order of battle, the concave inclining outward! Her tusks rattled away like the castinets of a negro minstrel, only the sounds were those of alarm, rage and defiance. Judging from her double battery of heavy guns, she must have left a large family at home while she went out to forage. You ought to have seen this "hunter" take to a tree! The movement showed timidity, and the enemy became emboldened thereby, and at once pushed the advantage aggressively. She came on sideways, like a hog for war! Every separate bristle stood straight up, like 1 o'clock!

"Piggy, piggy, poor old piggy," I exclaimed, in the most seductive tones I could get through my chattering teeth. But the fiend was proof against such gentle blandishments, and moved on my works, slowly but determinedly. She was now within a few feet of my tree, with the foam dropping from her champing jaws!

Well, beloved reader, I did what many a brave man has done before, in the face of overwhelming odds. I took to my heels through the woods! With fierce grunts of triumph, the enemy came on in pursuit. A limb knocked off my hat, and another nearly knocked out an eye. But true courage is not disconcerted by trifles, and my short legs did their duty manfully. The " time " I made, notwithstanding the bad condition of the track, is a marvel to me even unto this day. In a little while the sounds of pursuit grew fainter and fainter, and at length entirely ceased. The victory was mine!

But I got lost in the woods, and wandered around for hours, in helpless bewilderment. Just as I was about giving out in utter despair, the sound of the great lake struck its joyous tones to my heart, and afforded me a clue through the labyrinth. I soon reached its welcome shore, and then knew my way.

I entered my home just after dark, hatless, clothes torn to tatters, and soaked, fore and aft, in blood by the brambles.

When I had related my adventure to the family, my wife, who is of an affectionate disposition, kindly complimented me as being the " biggest fool in the settlement!"

" You're a pretty hunter, *you* are," she continued, " don't know a hog from a deer!"

Sympathetic reader, the tracks of the two distinct animals are very similar to an unpracticed eye, only that of the grown swine is much the largest. But then, you see, I thought the deer I was after was such a thundering *big* fellow! Pray excuse the mistake.

MY MAPLE.

IT stands right against the little western window of my cabin, does the maple tree of which I write. How the fierce fire spared it in its hunger, that time the clearing was first burned over, and log, and limb, and underbrush shrank into ashes in an instant, is yet an unsolved mystery to the mind untutored in wild western phenomenon. But here it stands, the sole remaining living representative of what was three years ago sixteen acres of primeval forest. The desolation was accomplished the year before I had left my eastern home to enter upon the forty acres of which this clearing is a part. My maple alone stands, untouched and vigorous, amid the charred and ashy desolation of its surroundings.

When the snows of the long northern winter have at last yielded to the encroachments of the later spring upon their sovereignty, how I love to sit and watch the swelling buds of my lonely maple, unfolding toward the green leaf, and to see their shadows deepening, day by day, upon the little carpet of white clover beneath. June comes in its season and brings my sturdy little maple a rich garniture of green, which the cunning dew drop loves to gather upon when the night comes on, to be burnished into diamonds by the morning sun. And then the little birds come from the far South, and seek out even here the homes of rude, uncultivated men, and awaken with music those old memories of other lands that so sadden the heart and purify the soul of the wanderer.

There was one little fellow—a very little fellow—who came early last Summer and took a squatter title to my maple.

And all the beautiful days would he hop from twig to twig,
peering under the leaves for tiny insects. Ah! has Nature,
in all her ways, no exception to the law of Destroyer and
Victim?

This little bird of mine is all over bottle green, except a
narrow clerical streak of white about his throat, and an un-
dertaker's patch of regulation mourning at the termination of
his tail. He has a keen, inquisitive little eye, that finds the
food that has just escaped the careless search of the restless
little wren—that belligerent marauder upon the bailiwick of
all the other feathered tribes, from hawk to humming-bird.

Sometimes my bird of the maple will hop out cautiously
to the very end of the limb nearest my window, within a few
feet of my manuscript, turn his little black eye curiously and
inquiringly into my face, as though he thought I must be
hungry, and in need of the still fluttering miller he holds in
his little bill.

One morning my little melodist brought a companion with
him from the forest, of his own kind, but of a soberer hue.
And wasn't that thereafter a happy couple! Side by side
in their leafy covert would they sit all the matin morning,
and sing and twitter lovingly to each other, dart at intervals,
like animated emeralds, into the sunlight, then back again
into their home by my window. All this was a new joy to
me. Dear reader, if you ever come to live alone in the
solemn wilderness, you will be glad to find companionship in
humble and unregarded things.

One day I noticed that my little friends were unusually
restless, as though agitated by the near pressure of some
important event. As I watched their amusing earnestness of
demonstration toward each other, they sallied off, and in a
few moments after I had resumed my writing, I was interrupted by a muffled twitter. Glancing at my maple, behold

my little friends, with each a shred of building material in
its bill! My birdies had been getting married and were pre-
paring for the consequences!

Well, the nuptial nest was finally completed, and Mrs.
Green did her duty in the premises. By poking my rifle
into the tree, and displacing a few interlaced branches, I was
rejoiced with a view of four dear little eggs of deep blue,
mottled with irregular brown spots. And upon these did
Mrs. Green sit, day by day, rarely leaving her maternal treasures, Mr. Green industriously bringing her the nicest fat
grubs that an adjacent sward afforded.

And wasn't little Mr. Green jolly! Hour by hour would
he sit

> " Atilt like a blossom, amid the leaves,
> And let his illumined being o'errun,
> With the deluge of summer it receives.
> His mate feels the eggs beneath her wings,
> And the heart in her dumb breast flutters and sings.
> He sings to the wide world and she to the nest.—
> In the nice ear of Nature, which song is the best?"

But I weary the impatient reader, and I fear but few others
peruse these musing vagaries of mine, and so I will not push
this picture to completion. A beautiful and instructive finale
remains undisclosed in the inner recesses of memory. Some
few souls of clearer mould wish I had proceeded, and to pun-
ish such for being less gross than their fellows, I drop my
birdies out of sight.

The summer by the Great Lake is gone, and taken with it
the beauty and the glory of clearing and forest. My eyes are
fixed tearfully upon my maple. Its branches are bare and
verdureless, save where here and there upon a moaning limb
a yellow and withered leaf clings to its sapless stem, as
though reluctant to go down to the cold and pitiless earth.

But even as I gaze, one by one these last lingering creations of the summer shower and sunshine drop silently downward, are caught up by the autumnal winds and eddied onward beyond the ken of my tearful vision.

And even thus from the tree˜of life have the companions of my boyhood passed into the oblivion of the grave. The summer sun comes and goes, my maple puts on and off its green garniture, but to the˙ associates of my youth there is no earthly resurrection. Good men tell us of a happy land beyond the dark river, where pain, nor death, nor sorrow never enter, and where the trees ever bloom by the waters of eternal life. Happy is he who has faith in these things, for to him Death is but the janitor who holds in trust the key of his eternal heritage.

ANOTHER INTERESTING INTERVIEW WITH THE "OLD SETTLER."

THE snow storm had lasted three days, and was still doing its best to hide from the eye of man all the work of his hands. The fences had disappeared. The drifts had environed the few cabins of the clearing, even to the eaves of the roof. The wreaths of smoke from the roaring fires beneath were scarcely discernible through the white siftings of the dark clouds, as the winds roared, and howled, and whistled, and screeched in the maddened play of the tempest. The mighty hemlocks swayed to and fro like drunken men, and the solemn moanings of the agonized lake mingled in the elemental convulsion, sounding like a dirge from eternity over a shaken and endangered world.

" Surely," said I, in a congratulatory mental expression, " mine adversary will not trouble me to-day, and the train of thought I am exercising for my pet new story will receive no fatal interruption from the thoughtless garrulity of my distant neighbor, the " Old Settler."

So thinking, and fortified by the thought, I seated myself at my little pine table, scattered around my last few sheets of paper one by one, that the whole entablature might have that slovenly literary appearance which is supposed to mark the indifference of transcendent genius to the graces of order; inked my pen to its hilt so that in drawing it back its contents might drop blots upon all its surroundings—which is also another mark—a black one—of the unaffected genius of your true romance writer; ran my finger through the bald

place on the top of my head, " where the hair used to grow ;"
put on the regulation frown, and the troubled look which
distinguishes our tribe when desirous of being " interesting"
in the sight of the *softer* sex, and then bent over to the work
before me, the initial chapter of my new "thrilling" story.

Imagination was propitious and poured out her wealth of
romance faster than my pen could invoice her generous
donations. Just as I had inked the entrance of the lovely
Georgiana Wilhelmina Jenkins upon the stage, leaning upon
the arm of Charles Augustus Henry de Leatherhead, a sound
outside my cabin sent my heated fancy down into the bulb of
zero.

"And my heart in its leap stood still, like a frozen waterfall!"

Yes, there was no mistaking either the song or the
singer, as these lines cut their way, sharp and ringing, through
the frosty air :

"I fought with General Sherman,
For the flag of Uncle Sam,
And we marched through Georgia
Just like a d———!"

It was the "Old Settler" that here lifted the latch and
stood before me, six feet three inches in his snow shoes !
"Kinder rough out this mornin' !" was his opening saluta-
tion. "Reckon your fellers what's a haulin' saw-logs down
by the old Ingun trail won't make morn'n a half day of it.
Oxen ain't worth much on a pull of forty inches of snow to
the square foot on a dead level, leavin' out the big drift at the
head of the gorge. Better go and tell 'em to call it half a
day, neighbor, or I'll be durned if them Norweegin scalawags
won't fool around there, makin' a big fuss, and doin' nothin',

and then charge for a hull day. You don't know them fur-
rin chaps that hev dropped down this way from the old country as well as you will after a while, and I don't want to see
you fooled out of your money by no sich. When you give
me that new hat last summer, when the 'tater bugs was doin'
their level best on a short notice, I made up my mind to look
out a little arter your interests."

I had thus far paid no attention to my tormentor, except a
cold nod of recognition at his entrance, but pretended to be
engaged in the hopeless task of continuing my writing. Observing that I made no response to his kindly suggestion in
reference to the men in my employ, he drew a chair toward
the stove, squirted a gill of tobacco juice upon that useful
servitor of a cold cabin, which instantly resented the indig-
nity by a fierce and prolonged hiss.

The Old Settler sat a few moments in meditative silence,
and then broke forth with:

"'Pears to me, mister, that you'm a leetle huffy this
mornin'."

"To tell you the truth, my friend," I rejoined, "you have
come in upon me just as I was engaged on a very particular
task of writing that I am anxious to finish to-day, and really
I cannot afford the time at present for that neighborly talk
that would be so agreeable under ordinary circumstances.
But to-day you will have to excuse me."

"Jes so, mister, jes so! Bizness afore pleasure is the sap-
lin' that's always safe to tie to. But it don't make the least
mite of difference to me. I kin talk jist as well to a feller
when he's a writin, as when he aint. The screechin' of that
pen of your'n don't flusterfy me a bit. I kin do pretty much
all the talkin' while you go on with the writin'."

I here resumed my work with wild determination, and the
Old Settler pulled forth a plug of real Virginia " niggar

head " from his pouch, shaved off a few slices with his hunting knife, filled his short dingy pipe, lit it, and puffed away for a few seconds in mollified silence. But a thought suddenly insisted upon utterance, and removing his pipe from his mouth he resumed his interruptions thus:

" Mister, I was over to Bear Lake last Sunday to set my otter traps, when I met Jim Huffman, who was goin' down to Shelby with a thunderin' big buck on his bob-sled, which he had popped over that mornin' at the lower licks. And Jim up and axed me what your fust name was, as he wanted to git the schoolmaster to write a letter for him about hirein' out to you to do that loggin' on the south side of your forty. What mout your fust name be? "

I threw myself back in my chair, and in a tone half indignant, half despairing, exclaimed:

" *Bored*! my first name is *Bored*! just at present."

The Old Settler replaced his pipe in his mouth, gave a few vigorous sucks by way of reviving its dying embers, mused a moment, and then said:

" Are you any a kin to the Bords down about Muskegon?"

This was about the last feather, and I could make no response. The Old Settler must have observed the despair of my expression, for he said, in a kindly and encouraging tone:

" Don't mind me, neighbor Bord. Go on with that job of writin'. It's jist the same to me if you talk back or don't talk back. I reckon I know what belongs to manners, and when a man is busy I don't expect him to strike his axe in a stump and set down on the log to talk on my account. That's Pete Higgins, that is, and I don't keer a dead coon for the best man livin', eny furder then civilty is concerned."

A new stratagem here suggested itself as a last resort to my painfully bewildered senses. I remembered that this imperturbable monster—this uncouth Hercules of the woods—had informed me on a previous occasion that he had learned to read a little while in the army. There was a bound volume of Littell's Living Age upon my table, and it might be possible to get him interested in some one of its pages. I pushed the book toward him, and with a seductive but false smile, spoke the horrible man, thus :

" My dear friend and neighbor, here is a book of many interesting facts. I know you cannot fail to become interested in it ."

My tormentor stretched forth his hairy, horny, brawny hand, and took the proffered volume, and I resumed my writing, hopeful that a diversion in my favor had at last been accomplished. But this hope soon proved to be

"Like the snowflake on the river,
A moment bright, then gone forever ! "

A grunt of dissatisfaction again called my attention from my manuscript to my visitor. I looked up. He had just finished spelling out the name upon the back of the book, and a look of unutterable contempt was fast spreading over his hard features. He pushed the volume back toward me with a gesture of disgust :

" Mister," he exclaimed, " the feller what writ that book is a durn'd eternal humbug ! ' Little Livin' Agee !!' The little agee may do well enough for them chaps in the East, what ain't got stuff enough about 'em to keep their backbones straight, and who a right smart Western wind would blow out of their boots, and snap their pipe-stem legs into inch pieces, but no little agee for me. When one of us fellers out here git anything onnateral we want it big, acordin' to the country.

" L-i-t-t-l-e livin' agee ! And had to go and write a book about a thing that was no great shakes, no how ! The poor

Yankee slink, there ain't man enough in him to face a wood-chuck. I'll bet all my winter's hunt that my old woman, who is now well onto sixty years, can take that chap by the back of the neck and snap his toe nails off!"

The old settler paused a moment, but the expression of disgust upon his face continued to deepen. He shook his head slowly from side to side, by way of emphasis to the contempt that was evidently gathering strength within him. At length he looked up, and seeing me in the attitude of despair, exclaimed:

"Go on with that writin', Mister. I can talk all day, and if all the *little* livin' agee chaps in the East was a writin' books right under my nose, it wouldn't make me forget a word what I wanted to say."

Again he stopped, again shook his head in a most dissatisfied manner, and grunted forth his suppressed indignation. His silence continued for several minutes, and observing that his eyes were closed, and the motion of his head had subsided into only an occasional jerk backward, I fancied that my tormentor had sought in sleep a temporary refuge from the painful consideration of a subject that had so disturbed him. I cautiously resumed my pen, and recommenced work upon my new story. But I had scarcely penned a dozen words, when he suddenly wheeled his chair around in front of me, and opened his oral battery with renewed vigor.

"I wonder if that slack-twisted Yankee cuss ever heard of the big shakin' agee? When I lived in Ingeeana I had it nigh onto 'leven months at a stretch. I ain't no child, to sniffle and whimper at what can't be helped, but *that* rather fetched me.

"Neighbor Bord, at the eend of the fust six months I hadn't meat enough on these bones to tempt a starved wolf, and I used to shake the children out of bed, some nights when it was extra bad, until at last the old woman hed to make 'em sleep on the floor, without any kivers. Every durned rag in the cabin, and all the deer skins, hed to be piled on me to keep me from freezin', and tied on with the clothes line at that !

"Well, I hadn't been able to earn a cent in all this time and at last everything in the house was eat up. And the children began to come around where I would be a mopin' when once in awhile I had an off day from the d—— shakes, and ask me for a piece of bread. And the oldest one looked wolfish-like out of his eyes, when the baby toddled near him. So my wife sed to me one day, ' Pete,' sed she, ' you've always been a good husband to me, except sometimes when I was cross myself, and unreasonable, but I know neither of us really meant it. But you ain't much stronger now than little Sis, and if splittin' shingle bolts was five dollars a cord, you couldn't earn a loaf of bread a week. But something must be done, or Pete will eat up the baby right before our eyes. I've been thinkin' about this until I've had to go out doors behind the cabin and have a good cry where none of you could see me. But this morning when I went out into the woods to see if I could't find a few late berries, I came across something that will fill the meal barrel, and get some pork, and perhaps a little tea and sugar for you. I won't tell you now, but in the morning, when you feel the shakes coming on, just let me know.'

"Well, friend Bord, this kind of cheered me up, but what on airth the old woman meant I couldn't begin to guess. But next mornin', just as daylight was breakin' into the clearing, I felt the old crawl agoin' up and down my back. I waked up my wife, and told her that I know'd that there was an old he shake a comin' on that would likely rattle all the bones out of my body.

"She to once helped me out of bed, and I made out to git on my poor old ragged trowsers that was too rotten to mend, and out of doors I staggered, leaning on her shoulder. We tottered on for about half a mile, stoppin' to rest once in awhile, till at last the old woman sed: .

"'Dear Pete, here's what the good Lord has provided for us in our great distress,' and she pointed to the top of a thunderin' big hickory tree, that was covered with jist the biggist crop of nuts that eny man ever laid his eyes on. The tree crotched out about fifteen feet from the ground, and then, for want sharpens a feller's wits, I began to see the whole thing like a flash.

"'But how am I to get up there?' says I.

"With that she stepped into the bushes and dragged out a ladder, which she had herself made out of two poles, and nailed some old shingles onto them about a foot apart. Then she raised it agin the tree, but it was almighty hard work for her, and it jist reached the place. Without another word I crawled up, and sat down in the crotch. The agee had just got to work, and in about ten minutes begun to put in the big licks!

"The way them nuts came rattlin' down about that time was wuth the best circus you ever seed!

"The old woman undertook to pick 'em up in her apron, but she soon give up the job, and skeeted from under with both hands spread over her head. In ten minutes there wasn't a dozen nuts left on that tree, and hardly a leaf either. At last the old woman sung out:

"'Pete, for mercy sake come right down! If you stay up there another minute the whole top will be shook off, all the way above your head, and drop down and mash you?'

"I looked up, and sure enough some of the biggest limbs was beginnin' to split off from the body! I seed at once that the ladder would be too slow work, so I grasped my arms around the tree as far as they would reach, shet my eyes, said a short grace, and slid!

"Mr. Bord, it was a shag-bark hickory, old as all creation, and as rough as they make 'em. I was about two seconds in reaching the ground, but when I struck bottom I hadn't nothin' on but what a fellow is born with, except one old deer-skin shoe. The rest of my riggin' hung along in patches, from the crotch of that old tree all the way down to the roots!

"'That arternoon the old woman and the three children had all them hickory nuts hulled clean, and they measured about five bushel. The next day a tradin' scow came down the Wabash for New Orleans, and tied up on shore near our cabin, to get wood. We got a dollar and a quarter a bushel for them nuts, in trade, and laid in a stock that kept our mouths a going for a month."

Here the Old Settler held up a moment, and fastened his sharp blue eyes upon my face, as if to read therein the amount of credulity, or degree of patience, with which his story was received. To tell the truth, and in spite of my previous indignation at his persistent annoyance, I had involuntarily become interested in his preposterous relation. Observing this he resumed, with an evident expression of satisfaction:

"Well, mister, what with pork and mollasses, and batter cakes fried in coon fat, I soon begun to pick up a little, and in less than a matter of two weeks the agee sort a gin out, and I could do a little potterin' about the clearin', and things seemed to look as if I was a goin' to come around all right agin.

"My wife had a kind o' hankerin' arter religion, though she hed never jined the church. Her mother hed been a sort of a Methodist, and though the old woman hed hed a mighty hard time of it with a wuthless drunken husband, she died happy, a prayin' of the Lord.

"So my wife sed to me one day, 'Pete,' sed she, 'you ought to be thankful that the Good Man has heered my prayers, and raised you, as it were, from the dead. There is a big revival a goin' on at the little church over to Squattersville, and let's you and me go to-night, and who knows but what we may both git the blessin'?

"Well, I hedn't hed a real genewine shake in four days; and so to please my wife, who was about the right kind of a critter arter all, if she did let that tongue of hern git rather loose sometimes, I told her I reckoned we'd better go, and see how the thing would work.

"And so when night come, I wrapped my old army blankit around my clothes—for I was patched from top to bottom, and really ashamed to be seen by meetin' folks—and away we went, the old woman a marchin' ahead, and I a follerin' arter her.

"When we got there, the service was jist commencin' and the minister guv out a tex, and sed: 'What cum ye out fur to see; a reed *shakin'* by the wind?'

"Now, stranger, mebbee I was wrong, but this sort a riled me. He looked right at me when he sed it, and I kinder thought it was a slur at my agee, which hed made me nearly as slim as a reed, and which the Lord knows I couldn't help. My wife seed I was gittin' mad like, and she pinched me to keep still.

"Well, in about fifteen minutes, as true as I'm a livin' sinner, I felt the agee comin' on me all to once, with a full head of steam! I tried to put on the brakes, but the durn'd thing was on the down grade, and was bound to make up fur the four days lost time. And the minister kept all the time a yellin' out, ' *What cum ye out fur to see ; a reed shakin' by the wind ?* '

"At last I hed to jist lay down in the pew and let her rip ! The old woman was scared nearly to death, and tried to git me up to take me out. But every time she tuck holt of me, I shook her hands off agin the side of the pew until every-thing cracked agin.

"The thing kept a gittin' wus and wus. Bimeby the house begin to shake, and the folks stared around, frightened like. Soon half the people fell down upon their knees and prayed for mercy. The preacher shouted louder than ever: ' *What cum ye out fur to see; a reed shakin' by the wind?* ' and sed thet the ' Lord wuz in the work ! '

"At last the chimbly—which the morter must hev been a gittin' a leetle rottin—cum a rattlin' down upon the ruff; and then the screamin' was awful among the wimmin and children, jist as ef they thought a passel of reglar wild Injins was around, a gunnin' fur scalps.

" Well, the minister was a good man, but he couldn't stand *everything*. When the chimbly kim a tearin' down, he jist jumped out over the top of the pulpit, and hollered :

"' Breethcrin', truly has Satan power on this yearth ! ' And then he broke fur the door, with the hull crowd a fol-lerin', and screechin' like mad.

" All to once Deacon Spooner happened to spy me a layin' on the floor as he ran by, and he stopped and sung out :

" ' Breethering and sistern, don't be skeert. It's nobody but Pete Higgins, a shakin' with the Wabash agee! '

" But the meetin' was busted up fur that night, and so was the revival fur the hull season.

" The old woman sort o' cussed me all the way home, jist as ef I could help it. But she was so ashamed to think what the hull neighborhood would say, that it made her onreasonable like, and as soon as her cussin' feelin's hed cooled off, she cried, and sed she was a fool, and that it was all her fault fur askin' of me to go.

"And now, mister," resumed the narrator of this strange story, after a few furtive glances at my countenance, " is it enny ways strange that I got riled when you tried to poke that yankee bummer's book onto me, about his *little* agee ! I don't know much in the way of larnin', but there aint no livin' man what kin give me a new wrinkle about the shakes."

And thus saying, the Old Settler shouldered his rifle, and with something of an injured and defiant air, strode out into the storm.

But the inspiration of the romance I had attempted went out long before he did, and may now be scored among things lost to earth.

THE VISION.

I AM sitting alone, my deary—
  Alone, and the rain patters down,
The world on the outside is dreary,
  And thick clouds hang over the town;
My pencil goes over the paper,
  My heart beats the bars of its cage,
And the light from the shade of my taper
  Shows a tear-drop or so on my page.

A feeling of sadness comes o'er me—
  A weakness of memories dear,
For the past, summoned up now before me,
  Sits you by the side of me here;
The light of your dark eye is gleaming,
  In mine with the love it once bore,
And the years from the mist of my dreaming,
  Loom up from eternity's shore.

Thy hand in my own, my once dearest—
  Thy kiss once again on my brow;
Come closer; what is it thou fearest?
  The danger is passed with us now:
The faith you once swore is now broken,
  And we in the world are alone—
And the words that can never be spoken
  Die out in my heart with a moan.

But yet with the vision I linger,
  Its shadowy form by my side—
The ring that I gave, on its finger,
  With the bud in its hair of a bride.
It fades as my arms reach to clasp it—
  It slowly dissolves into air,
And the hope that went out to grasp it,
  Gives place to the gloom of despair!

I am sitting alone now, my deary—
  Alone, and the rain patters down,
The world in the darkness is dreary,
  And footsteps have ceased in the town;
My pencil glides over the paper,
  My heart beats the bars of its cage,
And the glow through the shade of my taper
  Reveals a tear-drop on my page.

JANE JERUSHA SKEGGS.

[The following nonsensical, but rather amusing verses, I wrote many years ago, for the Trenton *True American*. I never heard of their being copied in any other journal in this country, but about five years afterward they came back across the Atlantic, in a London periodical called "The Ladies Own," as original. Of *course* they then went the "grand rounds" in the land of their birth. Truly a "poet," like a prophet, has no honor in his own country.]

IT is many years since I fell in love
  With Jane Jerusha Skeggs,
The prettiest piece of calico.
  That ever went upon legs.

By meadow, and creek, and wood, and dell,
  So often we did walk!
And the moonlight smiled on her tempting lips,
  And the night winds learned our talk!

Jane Jerusha was all to me,
  For my heart was young and true,
And I loved with a double and twisted love,
  And a love that was honest, too!

I roamed all over the neighbors' farms,
  And robbed the wildwood bowers,
And tore my trousers and scratched my hands,
  In search of the fairest flowers!

In my holy love I brought all these,
  To my Jerusha Jane,
But I wouldn't be so foolish now,
  . If I was a boy again!

A city chap came along one day,
  All dressed up in store clothes,
With a shiny hat and a shiny vest,
  And a mustache under his nose!

He asked her to go to singing school,
  (For her father owned a farm,)
And she left me, her country love,
  And took the new chap's arm!

And all that night I never slept,
  Nor could I eat next day,
For I loved that girl with a fervent love,
  That nought could drive away!

I strove to win her back to me,
  But it was all in vain;
The city chap with the hairy lip,
  Married Jerusha Jane!

And my poor heart was sick and sore,
  Until the thought struck me,
That just as good fish still remained,
  As those caught in the sea!

So I went to Methodist Church one night,
  And saw a dark brown curl,
Peeping out from under a gypsy hat—
  Well, I married that very girl!

And many years have come and gone,
  And I think my loss my gain,
And I often bless that hairy chap,
  Who stole Jerusha Jane!

A TWO DOLLAR VISIT FROM THE "OLD SETTLER."

I WAS really pleased to see him this time. He had been working in a lumber camp up on the Pere Marquette for six weeks past, and had come home to keep Christmas. Being about my only visiting neighbor, I felt his long absence to be a deprivation. The most unpromising companionship is a relief to one's loneliness in these regions, in the long winter season, when the deep snow coops one up in his cabin, with no resources either of amusement or labor. And so I gave him a truly cordial greeting, as he stepped over my threshold, and with a genial smile illuminating his rugged features, wished me a " Merry Christmas, neighbor !"

After relating to me some of his trivial adventures in the woods during the winter, the Old Settler stepped to a corner of the cabin, picked up my beautiful " Wesson" rifle, and examined it critically.

" This 'ere gun of yourn," he remarked, " is a pretty thing to look at, but aint of no airthly account up this way. It carries about three hundred to the pound, and you might put fifty of them little blue pills into a right fat bear without tetchin' a wital part. A good stiff side wind would wary one of them balls six inches to the twenty rod. It may be a nice enough plaything for children, to them as kin afford it, but for real shootin' it ain't worth the powder to blow it to ―――― !"

I apologized for the offending weapon, on the ground that

it was used in the East simply for target practice among fancy sportsmen.

After a few minutes more spent in ordinary conversation, I managed to get the Old Settler upon the subject of his interesting experiences as a hunter in these wilds, one or two of which I have concluded to preserve in this volume.

"About ten years ago, neighbor," he commenced, "there was a store clothes feller cum in here from Shikago for a hunt. His father owned the shingle mill at Pentwater, and that's the way he happened to drift into these parts. As mine was the only cabin on the Pint, he hed to bunk in with me. He hed plenty of money, and was to pay me two dollars a day for my old jackass and me to go a hunting with him. Neighbor Bord, the woods was full of deer in them days, and we hed a way of huntin' 'em at nights, which is called 'shinin' their eyes.' I kin ony 'splain it to you this way. Ef you ever looked under a house, or a barn, when there was a cat, or a skunk, or any such varmint under there in the dark, you could see nothin' ony two great shiney eyes, what looked like balls of fire.

"Well, us hunters used to go out in the woods a nights, hevin' a long handle fryin' pan, and when we got to the right place we would light a fire in the pan, and one feller would carry it around on his shoulder, while the rest on us would foller on behind, with our rifles ready in our hands. As soon as we cum near a deer, the cuss would stop, astonished like, and look right at the blaze. Then we could see two great eyes shinin' in the darkness, and takin' aim right between them, was almost sartin to kill. We always tuck my old jackass, which I brought out with me from Injeeana, along, to bring home the deer, ef we shot enny.

"Well, the fust night me and the store clothes feller, and the jackass, went out, this wus what happened: Of course he wanted to do the shootin', and so I hed to carry the pan. When we got to the feedin' ground, we tied the jackass to a tree, lit our fire, and took a circle around. We hed pushed around for ten minutes or so, when all to wunst the store clothes feller sung out 'stop!' I looked up, and there within ten paces was two great starin' balls of fire. I know'd what it all ment at the fust glance, but before I could holler for him to hold on, 'bang!' went his durned old musket, and let out about a handful of buckshot! There was one onairthly bray, that fairly shook the trees all around, and made the air shudder like, and when I run up, there lay my poor old jackass, a kickin' of his last kick!

"Well, neighbor, I cussed that feller out of seventy-five dollars for that jackass, which he wusn't wuth twenty, but then I was so infarnally mad that I didn't adzacly know what I was doin'. He left next mornin' at daylight, and I've never heern tell on him since."

I laughed heartily, at the climax of this story, and the "Old Settler" seemed mightily tickled at the way I enjoyed it. I stepped to the closet and handed him three or four first rate Havana segars, and invited him to take a smoke. He accepted them with an expression of thanks, craunched them up fine in his huge paw, consigned the mass to his tobacco pouch, filled a short dirty pipe, and puffed away a few moments in silence. At last he said:

"I b'lieve I never told you about shootin' that bear, two years ago last winter? I told it to a newspaper chap what I met at a tavern down to Grand Rapids, and he said he would put it in print, and send me a paper, but I reckon he must hev forgot. Leastwise I never heerd anything from him since.

"One day I was a burnin' brush in the clearin', when I seed about a thousand crows, a dartin' in and out of the top of a big hemlock, and keepin' up the awfullest squallin' you ever heerd. I to wunst knowed there was somethin' up more'n common. And so I picked up my gun—and I've got the same gun yit—and started for the tree. I worked around among the bushes ontil I got within about twenty rod of where the rumpus was, and on peepin' out, sure enough there sot up in the highest crotch, an all fired big bear, a real four hundred pounder. Fust one crow would dart in on him, and then a half a dozen would foller, and he kept a boxin' at 'em right and left, as savage as a wild Ingin. The bear was so busy a watchin' and fightin' them crows, which kept up the cussedest noise all the time, that he never looked anywhere else. I crawled up to about eight rod of the tree, the bear all the time a strikin' out, fust at one crow, and then at another, without ever wunst suspectin' of any other danger. Bime by I got tired of watchin' the fun, and so I took aim jist below the old feller's shoulder, and tetched the hair trigger! You ought'er seen him come down, head foremost, all in heap like! He din'nt even kick nary time after he struck the ground. *And, mister, that durned fool of a bear thinks to this day it was them crows what killed him!* And I've got the same gun yit!"

At the conclusion of this interesting recital, the "Old Settler" started up and declared that he must be going. As he reached the door he stopped, turned around, put his hand searchingly in his pocket, and exclaimed:

"O, mister, I lik'd to hev forgot. I borrered three dollars off of you to pay my taxes. I've got a five dollar bill here, and ef you'll jist hand me the change we'll settle that little matter."

Delighted at this exhibition of unexpected honesty, on the part of one I had so mistrusted, I opened my pocket-book, and at once handed him the two dollars. He grabbed the amount with one hand, and continued to fumble in his pockets with the other. A last he turned a worried and perplexed look upon me, scratched his shaggy head, and said :

"Durn my skin ef my old woman hain't and went and tuck that five dollar bill out of my pocket when she was a mendin' of my coat this mornin'! But never mind, neighbor. I'll be along agin in a day or two, and step in and hand it to you. But I don't like sich tricks, and when I git to home, I'll be apt to raise particular thunder around the cabin, mind I tell you! I don't keer so much about it, ony for the looks of the thing. It's mortifyin' to be fooled in this way, but I'll make it all right when I cum a long next time !"

And so saying the "Old Settler" shook his head two or three times, indignantly, at the thought of the trick his "old woman" had played upon him, and walked off two dollars richer then when he entered. He hasn't found it convenient to call with that five dollar bill yet !

THE DESERTED CABIN.

A TALE OF NORTHERN MICHIGAN.

"I KNOW pretty much all about it," said the hunter, "and if you wish to hear the story, we will sit down upon this old hemlock log while I relate it."

We had been on the trail of a herd of deer all day, without being able to secure a shot, when late in the afternoon we came upon a log cabin within sight of the shores of Lake Michigan. The low roof had fallen in, the blackberry and the raspberry had rooted in the earth between the logs, and decay and dilapidation marked all its immediate surroundings. But there were faint traces of former flower beds before the door, and here and there a vine of beauty and of bloom struggled through the thick weeds, and entwined themselves around the solitary ruins. A woman of taste and culture had evidently planted and tended these, and it was the conviction of this fact, so rare in this lonely wilderness, that prompted me to ask the hunter if he knew ought of its history. His response is the commencement of this tale, and he continued as follows:

"It was twenty years ago—long before the cabin of a single white settler had been built upon the lake shore, all the way between Pentwater and Grand Haven—when I first saw this cabin. Chippewa and Ottawa Indians held all the vast country between White River and Lake Superior, and roamed these forests in pursuit of game. Father and I had been up in the Grand Traverse country trapping otter and shooting deer and bear. Early in the spring we loaded the canoe with our peltries, and commenced paddling along the the lake shore for Chicago, three hundred miles distant. Toward evening on the fourth day down, a tremendous blow came up out of the northwest. In the far distance we could see the huge waves bearing down upon us, the first one of which would have dashed us to destruction the moment it reached our little vessel. But we were but about twenty paddle strokes from the shore, and we soon had our boat and its treasures high up on the sandy beach.

"Stranger, did you ever see old Michigan when angered by a hurricane? Well, it's a bully thing to look upon from a land point, but woe to the ships and sailors who are then upon its waters! The treacherous old termagant is peaceful now, and her bosom heaves as gently as that of an infant in its slumbers. I have seen it thus a hundred times, and then within an hour it would begin to seethe, and boil, and foam, all the waters of its great depths seeming to be scooped up into mountains, and hurled one at the other by the winds in their fury. I have seen the clouds come down until they formed a perpendicular wall, whose base rested upon the waters and its summit against the sky. And all along, where it rested upon the lake, it was broken into great caverns, whose horrid mouths looked like the black entrances to eternal perdition. And all this comes with but a moment of preliminary warning, and that is the reason why old Michigan swallows up more vessels yearly than the Atlantic and Pacific oceans combined, and the dead of her mighty depths are skeletoned from Mackinaw to Chicago. You may walk her eastern shore for two hundred miles with a wreck always in sight. But I am running away from my story.

"Well, on securing our canoe we walked around and soon discovered a wreath of smoke curling up from among the dark hemlocks of the dense forest that lined the coast. We took it for granted that this was an encampment of Indian hunters; but as the Chippewas and Ottawas have always been treated kindly by our people, we had no fears for the safety of ourselves or property. So we pushed at once in the direction of the smoke, and in less than ten minutes came upon this very cabin, whose silent ruins are now before us.

"A huge deerhound offered a snarling resistance to our approach, which brought to the door a man and a woman, whose appearance startled me into a sort of awe, so strangely different were they from any human beings I had ever looked upon before.

"I was but twelve years of age, born in the wilderness, and had never seen any other kind of people than the rude white and red hunters on the outer verge of civilization. The man was apparently about twenty-five years of age, with fair complexion, dark hair and eyes, heavy mustache, and the rest of his face cleanly shaven. His clothes were of fine texture, wonderfully neat, and fitted to his well-built form in a manner that excited my wonder and 'astonishment. He wore a ring upon his finger that sent forth dazzling flashes of light, and a heavy gold chain led from a vest button-hole to his watch pocket.

"The woman could not have been over eighteen, and her glossy brown hair fell carelessly down about a face of such wonderful beauty, so sad and yet so resigned, that as I gazed a feeling came over me as if I had been in the instant translated to another world. I had heard an old Catholic missionary among the Indians of the Pere Marquette country describe the saints and angels of Heaven, and now before me was a realization of what he had drawn. Boy as I was, whose little life had been passed in the woods among the most reckless and desperate men, and who never knew a

I·

mother's tenderness nor a sister's love, a holy feeling of prayer and worship flowed into my soul as I looked upon the vision before me.

"My father was an ignorant man—could neither read nor write—but as brave and fearless of danger as any one that ever lived. He had seen his father and mother killed and scalped by the Iroquois of Canada, and was himself hurried off into captivity by the band, and remained three years with the devils before opportunity for escape was presented.

"In the woods every man's cabin is every other man's home, be he comrade or stranger, to enter without knocking, remain without invitation, and depart without thanks. But the old man was painfully abashed in the presence of these superior beings. On the invitation to enter, kindly and hospitably spoken, he awkwardly snatched off his coonskin cap, made a most ridiculous attempt at a bow to the lady, tried to hide his rifle behind him as though it was out of place in such company, and behaved in so grotesque a manner, that, forgetting my own awe for a moment, I burst out in a peal of laughter. The young lady comprehended the cause at once, caught the contagion, and in spite of every effort at restraint, added her own silvery strains of mirth to the hilarious temptation. This instantly brought my father back to his independent manhood, and giving me a look that plainly presaged my future punishment, strode erect and confident into the cabin.

"After supper the stranger took father out into the little clearing to ask his opinion about some contemplated improvement. As soon as they were gone, the lady came and sat down by me, and plied me with questions all about my history, mode of life, and future intentions. As I look at these crumbling logs, so silent and yet so full of speech to me, I fancy I can see her as she sat right in yonder corner, twenty years ago, with her dark blue eyes fastened upon my boyish face, so full of a tender interest I could not understand, while her sweet womanly voice—so unlike anything I had ever heard or fancied—poured forth the consolations of a sympathy I had never known from a human being before. Stranger, you are looking at my eyes, I am not ashamed of their moisture.

"On the return of father and the stranger, the lady approached the latter and said :

"'George, I want you to go out and fasten up that jessamine for me. The wind is abroad upon the lake and will be here in all its fury soon. The gentlemen will please remain until we return.'

"They were gone perhaps ten minutes. On re-entering the cabin, the man at once asked father if he would let me remain with them for one year. He expected to be away a good part of the time, and needed some one to do the little work required during his absence. He could not think of leaving his wife all alone in such a place. He would pay well for the service. Then the lady came up, and putting her beautiful little hand upon father's huge shoulder, and looking up into his hard, brown face, with a smile that could win anything without words, said :

"'You will let the lad stay with me, please, sir?'

"My father was rough on me sometimes, for his had been a hard life, and he was very easily angered. Once when I missed a bear at fifteen rod, he ran at me, and with his flat hand struck me on the side of the head, and sent me sprawling to the ground fully ten feet from him. And then the flash of his resentment went out in shame and repentance, and he hastened to me, and gathered me up in his great arms, and pressed me to his bosom, and cried, and cursed himself

for a cowardly villain. My father loved me. He had nothing else to love.

"When the girl made this appeal, the man stepped up,
and taking a handful of gold from his pocket, said :

"'I will give you one hundred dollars for the boy's services for one year, and will pay you right here in advance.'

"My father drew himself up with a dignity and haughti-
ness I had never seen him exhibit before.

"'I will not sell my child,' he replied, 'for all the gold
that was either honestly or *dishonestly* come by. I have tried
to say no to this woman, but cannot. I am an ignorant man,
and have always lived in the woods. But I know that this
is no place for her, and that she is troubled at heart. The
boy may remain, but neither he nor me will touch your
money. He can earn nothing here but his food and clothing.
To *her* care I leave him.'

"The man turned pale at this speech, and his brow darkened, but he said nothing. My father looked him steadily in
the eye for a full minute, turned slowly around, shouldered
his rifle, and without looking at me, or bidding us good-bye,
strode out into the forest in the direction of the lake, and I
never saw him more. I may tell you of his tragic death on
some other occasion.

"My new situation gave me new ideas of life, and awakened in me an ambition that had never before entered into
my thoughts. The lady loved me as if I was a lost brother,
unexpectedly restored. I feel certain now that when she first
saw me she traced a resemblance to some dear one in her old
home in the far east. She soon taught me to read and write ;
talked to me of the lowly born and neglected who had risen
from obscurity in her own land, and won by the force of
their genius wealth, fame, power, and the respect of a nation.
My youthful mind drank with eagerness at this new fountain.

She had books of the lives of statesmen, of the discoveries of science, the theories of philosophers, the musings of poets. Boy that I was, with a mind heretofore tutored only to the chase, many of these things bewildered me, but I felt that my intellect was being strengthened by the discipline of thought, and I thirsted for further discoveries in the world of knowledge. My preceptress was overjoyed at my progress. Poor soul;—but few so good, so beautiful, so patient in a hidden sorrow, ever so needed one source of happiness.

" She never spoke to me of the past, and never uttered any complainings of the present. The man was very kind and loving toward her, but I knew that he had wronged her in some way, and I fairly hated him under this suspicion. Many and many a time have I caught her in tears, which she vainly strove to hide, and I often felt my own heart breaking over a sorrow I could not comprehend or alleviate.

" I have said these two cultivated beings, evidently of some great city, but now isolated in a cold and inhospitable wilderness as if they alone were the inhabitants of the world, loved each other. If you had seen them as I did, walking in the forest paths, or along the beach of the mighty lake when the summer moon was at its full, with the soft waves breaking mournfully but musically at their feet, you would have witnessed those sweet and tender endearments that are born only of love in young hearts, ere years and the realities of life harden into formality and selfishness.

" I had been in my new home about six months, when the man began to absent himself at longer and longer periods, often remaining away two weeks at a time. And the poor lady would do nothing but weep when the day of his appointed return passed without his coming. She grew thin and haggard, and a strange light began to gleam in her eyes. For on each return the man became more and more gloomy, and at times his irritation vented itself in harshness to the being he called wife.

"It was early in September, toward the close of a lovely day, when the man walked into the cabin from an unusually long absence, and sat down moodily, with scarce a word of recognition to either of us. The girl staggered toward him, fell upon her knees, and clasping her arms about his neck, while her wealth of hair almost buried his face and fell upon his shoulders, sobbed like one lost to all hope. The man rudely loosened her loving clasp, and arose to his feet. She lowered her head upon the vacated chair for a moment, sprang up, placed her hands upon his shoulders, and putting her sweet face close to his, said, in a low, soft, tremulous voice:

"' *Walter Danton, take me home to my mother!*'

"The man again repulsed her, and this time with an oath.

"' 'Then I will go alone!' she exclaimed, and in her loose white dress, and all bonnetless, she turned and passed out over the threshold for the last time. I noticed the wild gleam in her eye as she went forth, and my heart stood still with terror.

"Fifteen minutes passed, when the man went to the door and peered uneasily around.

"' 'Great God of mercy!' he fairly shrieked, 'she is gone!'

"And then he shouted 'Mary! Mary!' and the hollow echoes sent back the words in mockery of his agony.

"And now, like a madman, he started for the lake. I followed in the instant, but he far outstripped me in the race. When I reached the edge of the forest I looked out upon the placid bosom of the waters. A quarter of a mile from shore was a skiff, whose sail had caught the breeze, and was making rapid headway. A white form stood erect in the stern, and waved a handkerchief in farewell to an object on the shore. I rushed down. Danton was on his knees, shrieking most piteously for the occupant of the boat to return. Then he ran out into the water, both arms raised imploringly, praying and blaspheming in his wild delirium.

" At this instant the boat of a fisherman rounded the point. The madman dashed toward it, dragged the old man out into the shallow water, flung himself into the skiff, and set its prow towards the receding object.

" The long level rays of the setting sun flashed upon the smooth waters, and lit up the scene with terrible distinctness. Drawn against the horizon of the wide waters was the ghostly form of the woman, still erect in the frail vessel, and the pursuer could be seen making frantic efforts to lessen the distance between them, while his imploring cries still reached us from the distance. The sun went down, and the twilight came on. The foremost boat was swallowed up in the gloom and the shadows, and the pursuing one was soon lost in the advancing darkness.

" ' It is a good hundred miles across to the Wisconsin shore,' said the fisherman, ' and the wind is coming down out of the north. Neither that man nor that woman will ever be seen alive again.'

" And they never were, nor dead either.

" And ever on the anniversary of that night, the fishermen say a skiff is seen far out upon the waters, with a white form erect in its bow, waving a farewell to a man who is making frantic gestures from the shore.

" And now, that my story is ended," said the hunter, in a husky voice, " we will push on for the licks."

I MEET MY FIRST "INGIN."

Lo! the poor Indian whose untutored mind,
Takes whiskey "straight," and "goes it" till he's blind !

[*Essayed by Pope.*]

IN this our broad county of Oceana, there can be found at this writing nearly two thousand Indians—the remnants of the warlike tribes who once occupied all the regions of the great lakes, and whose history is so stained with horrible atrocities upon the earlier white settlers. My cabin stands right in the locality where Tecumseh, and Pontiac, his brother and prophet of the tribe, rallied the red warriors of the wilderness for a last struggle against the steady advances of the white invader. There is an old Indian trapper now living at Pere Marquette, in the county adjoining us on the north, who made one of the expedition that had such a fatal termination at the battle of the Thames, in what is now the State of Indiana. Col. Richard M. Johnson, afterwards Vice-President of the United States, commanded a regiment of Kentucky mounted rifles in that bloody struggle and slew Tecumseh in a hand-to-hand encounter. The facts of this incident of the battle may be of interest to our younger readers.

It was toward the close of that fearful contest, when the centre of the British order of battle had been broken by a desperate charge of Col. Johnson's regiment, and the demoralized Indian allies on either wing had fled and took to the woods, and got behind trees to fight in their own fashion, that Tecumseh met his fate. Johnson was desperately wounded in the victorious charge, and the splendid blooded mare he rode was fairly riddled with bullets. The brave Colonel, feeling her reeling under him, turned her head toward a fallen tree, when in rounding the top he found himself confronted by a stalwart savage, whose painted face was rendered more hideous by the blood that streamed down from a deep sword gash on the top of his uncovered head. The chieftain was in the act of ramming down a bullet when the two confronted each other, but the weapon had become so fouled from frequent discharges during the battle that the ball could not be sent home. The savage threw the rifle from him, and with a yell of hate and rage that would have paralyzed the nerves of a less brave antagonist, seized his tomahawk and hurled it at his enemy. But at the same instant Col. Johnson snatched his remaining pistol from its holster, and pulled the trigger full at the broad breast of the herculean warrior. Tecumseh, who was making a dash for his enemy, stopped, staggered for a instant, stooped down, groping blindly for his rifle, then drew his majestic form up straight to the perpendicular, uttered a loud yell of defiance, sprang upward into the air, and came down upon his face—dead. At the same instant the gallant mare sank slowly upon her haunches, swayed a moment, and rolled over with her rider, and died with a few feeble struggles. It was afterwards ascertained that she was pierced with sixteen bullets.

The tomahawk of the Indian had struck Col. Johnson between the thumb and forefinger of his bridle hand, and crippled it for life. With his other wounds, he was now helpless, and lay beside his dead favorite, until discovered by some of his men, and carried off the field of carnage.

It seems, my beloved, though possibly indignant reader, that I can never keep this erratic brain of mine to its prescribed and appointed task. When I sat down to my rough pine table a few minutes since to indite this sketch, I had no thought that my poor pen would scribble itself into the historical incident it has just recorded from memory. I inked it with a view to humor. It has strayed into a foughten field, and returned in blood.

Did you ever know a man, however deficient in voice or tune, who did not rather incline to the opinion that he was a pretty fair singer? He may so far doubt his endowment in the gift musical as to avoid experimenting in public, and to decline importunities to vocalize for the entertainment of a social party; but when that chap gets by himself in the solitude, where no man is, or is not suspected to be, he will give mouth to some favorite song of his, until the echoes mock him back in agony. I have been caught myself in the delusion that there was no listener, when a man, or a woman, or both together, would turn a clump of bushes suddenly upon me, and then for the first time a sense of the horrible discord I was forcing into the surrounding space would assail my better judgment, and mortification would set in at once. To be honest with you, the subscriber can neither sing or whistle the simplest tune to save his life, or his beloved country from a war with Spain. But in the weakness of his vanity he has at times thought otherwise, been caught in the act, paid the penalty in the derision of involuntary listeners, and the following incident is a case in point:

One day in the early October of the past year, when the first kiss of the dainty frost spirit had caused a crimson blush to overspread the fair face of the maple by my window, and the beeches in the ravine below turned yellow with envy, I wandered far out into the forest, to enjoy the luxurious lassitude which is nowhere so soothing as in the wilderness solitude by the northern waters of Lake Michigan. The winds had retired to their caves, the trees stood transfixed in the breezeless silence, and not a leaf showed the pulsation of life. I leaned against a huge hemlock, that was first rooted centuries before Columbus unfolded his dreams of a New World to Mr. and Mrs. Ferdinand of Spain. The magnificent magnitude of my dear country stole gradually into my meditations, and as my patriotism began to swell, and fret, and foam for outward expression, I seized, with a fearful roar, " The Sword of Bunker Hill," and knocked the solemn silence into fits in an instant.

I had got about half through this melodious tribute of gratitude to our " patriot sires and grandsires ˌhoary," when I heard a voice, saying :

" My white brother sings like a government mule !"

No bullfrog ever cut short his hoarse croakings quicker, at the sudden descent of a schoolboy's brickbat, than did the singer—I myself—at this frightful interruption ! In much trepidation, I turned my head, and there, within ten feet, stood a vision whose appearance was enough to startle a strong minded woman—or any other man—from the inherent courage of his nature. Lo! a poor Ingun stood before me, in all the panoply of a red warrior of the wilderness !

But the chieftain did not exactly realize my idea of the traditional Indian I had read of in my earlier days of youth and romance, of whom Cooper's aboriginal heroes were the types. On the contrary quite the reverse. This Lo's appearance would hardly do for high. His coat looked as if he was on the way to a paper mill. His shirt looked as if it had been washed in a swill barrel and dried on a gridiron. There had evidently been divers and sundry quilting frolics on the seat of his breeches. There was an irruption of black, bristly hair out of the crater of his crownless hat. In short, all his externals indicated the gentleman and the scholar, and a man who had seen better days.

Forcing an easiness of manner that I was far from feeling,
I approached the apparition, and extending my hand exclaimed :

"Philosopher of the woods, how fares it with thee to-day?"

> "The chieftain round him drew his cloak, (only he hadn't any,)
> Folded his arms and thus he spoke : "

"White man, if you call me a grasshopper of the woods,
Ingun put a head on you !"

I was a mile from home, and unarmed. The offended
chieftain held a rifle in one hand, and a recently killed skunk
in the other. My offence was rank, and smelled to Heaven.
So did the skunk.

I do not think I would have blanched before his rifle, for
I had been a warrior myself, per a six hundred dollar substitute, in the war of the rebellion. But the sight of that
skunk, and the odor in which he was enpanoplied, suggested
diplomacy. A happy precedent had been elaborated by
divers of the present congress. I will try a little *credit mobilier* upon this representative of his people.

With me, action follows resolve, even as the thunder booms
upon the lightning. I drew forth my pipe, matches, and
tobacco pouch. The irate barbarian shook his head, and also
his skunk likewise.

Then in my other pocket did I explore, and brought out
a beautiful four bladed knife.

I saw a sign of relenting in his dark eye, trimmed though
it was with lids the edges of which looked like red ferreting·

He laid down his rifle, but advanced a step nearer with his
skunk, and swung it around, as I have seen a censor swung
at a religious ceremony. Only the effect was different.

If I must die, I preferred the rifle.

But one more *credit mobilier* argument remained. I pulled out my pocket-book, and laid its last greenback upon the heap of peace offerings.

"It is well," said the chieftain, as he "raked in the pile," "and my white brother can depart in peace to his kindred. The wife of Come-It-Strong is weeping in his lodge ; for the venison is all eaten, and the fire-water is as the early dew which the sun drinketh up, and it is not. The gifts of my white brother are to my heart like the strong drink that cometh from Chicago, and which eateth through the staves of the barrel."

Overcome by his unwonted emotions, the child of Nature lifted the skunk to his eyes,

"And wiped away a tear!"

He then put straight out into the forest, like a green-tailed fly from a sugar house.

Dearly beloved, your correspondent is not singing so much in the woods as he used to !

THE SPECTRE OF THE HEMLOCK GORGE.

A T any time it was a place to be avoided by persons of average imagination, or superstitious inclinings. But it was a very careless or a very courageous foot that would willingly enter upon its paths when the night had come down upon its natural gloom and unbroken solitude.

The gorge was not over one hundred feet in width, but gazed into from the low ridge on either side, the effect was anything but pleasant and inspiring. The great trees that grew up from its depths scarcely raised their tops to the outer surface, and their density gave a darkness to noonday beneath. These trees were all of the gloomy hemlock. The sojourner amid the forests of Northern Michigan can now easily understand the lonely and awe-inspiring features of the gorge into which I am attempting to lead my readers.

It ran parallel to the Great Lake, and but a short distance from its moaning and troubled waters. And when the winds were out in their fury, and swept through the gorge with irresistible and invisible wings, the roar that came up from its depths, and went out into the surrounding forest, almost silenced the great waves that broke upon the adjacent shore.

Is it any wonder, then, that the traditions of the few scattered settlers had invested the spot with ghostly disembodied spirits, whose shrieks added to the horrors of the midnight tempests?

The gorge was of easy entrance on the south, but difficult of egress on the north. A narrow deer path ran through it, but few were the hunters who cared to tread its dark maze in pursuit of game. The experiment had been tried by one or two of the few adventurers who occasionally came down from the islands of the upper lake, when the deer and bear had been driven southward by the Ottawa and Chippewa bands, in their annual expeditions from St. Marie and Huron. But it is said that none of such adventurers ever passed out at the other extremity, but quickly returned with mortal fear de_ picted upon their faces. Even the gaunt, fierce Indian wolf dogs came howling out in advance of their retreating masters, with blood-shot eyes and piteous whines that told of super-natural alarms.

These facts had been so generally related to me by the set-tlers, that at last my ridicule at the idea gave place to a desire to learn from some more intelligent source, or by personal ex-ploration, the true basis of this local superstition.

I could not venture alone without danger of getting lost, and I was hardly prepared to let any one of my three more immediate neighbors into the secret of a curiosity, that argued a sort of half-defined credulity of which I was really ashamed.

And so the matter rested until the beautiful northern sum-mer had past, and the early November snows came down softly upon the earth, and covered the autumnal leaves with a garment of purity and beauty.

The subject of the gorge and its mystery had almost lost their hold upon my curiosity, when one afternoon the hunter —he who had told me the story of the deserted cabin— chanced to be passing by. I hailed him and he walked in. He informed me that he was on his way to the old trapping grounds near the head of the lake, on the Wisconsin side, in which neighborhood he expected to pass the winter. I in-vited him to stay all night and take a fresh start in the morn-ing. He modestly accepted the suggestion, observing that he had walked about thirty miles since daylight, and as the snow had hidden the smaller logs of the forest, pushing his way over and among them was difficult and toilsome work, and that he really felt tired and exhausted.

In due time a smoking supper of broiled venison and roasted potatoes—bread being among one of the occasionals of my wilderness home—was ready to be disposed of, and with glorious appetites, braced by abstinence since morning, we two drew up to the table, and silently thanking the Giver of all good, proceeded to feast upon His bounties. These fully indulged in, but without gluttony, prepared us for a pleasant evening of social intercourse, and a sound and in. vigorating sleep when weary eyelids droop responsive to a law of nature.

Day had now renounced its sceptre to the hand of dark- ness, and the night drew its shadows around our little world without, until neither wood or clearing could be distinguished in the more remote distance. We drew our chairs to the bright and cheerful fire, filled our pipes, and conversed for a while on the usual indifferent subjects of local gossip. These exhausted, I at last ventured to inquire of my usually silent, but intelligent visitor, in reference to the dreaded gorge and its accredited mystery.

The hunter looked up at me with a quick movement, as if to observe if my request was a jesting one, or instigated by a real interest in what most men of reading and observation would at once set down as an idle and absurd tale, hatched in the undisciplined imagination of ignorant and superstitious woodmen. Then, with the faintest evidence of a smile play- ing around his mouth, he remarked :

"And so you have heard of the hemlock gorge, and what is generally believed to be, here among the settlers, its ghostly inhabitant? Well, you will doubtless laugh at my strange recital, as I would myself if, unknowing the facts, I listened to them from the lips of another."

Here the hunter took a few vigorous whiffs at his pipe by way of finishing its contents, knocked out the ashes, returned it to his pouch, and began :

" A dozen or so years ago, before the hundreds of Chicago lumbermen came into these parts, deer and bear abounded in great numbers, and this section of the lake shore was considered by hunters and trappers as one of the best for their calling in all Northern Michigan.   There was not a single permanent settler for many miles around, and not a ten acre clearing in all which is now called Benona Township.

"I used to come out here then every winter, with a single comrade and partner.   He was a Canadian-Frenchman named LeClerc, and the most cunning hunter and trapper I ever met with, and that is saying a great deal in his favor.   He seemed instinctively to understand the habits, and the lurking places of all the animals of the water and the woods, and he would follow the trail of other hunters, who would go miles without seeing horn, hoof, or hide, and LeClerc would return laden with the trophies which had entirely escaped their keenest observation.

" But the old man was terribly profane, both in his native and acquired language.   But for swearing he always seemed to prefer the French, until the supply was exhausted, and then he would replenish his impoverished vocabulary by copious draughts upon the hardest English expletives.

" But he was a truly brave veteran of the woods, and as warm-hearted and sympathetic as a woman, in any emergency that appealed to tenderness.   He finally died, his broken rifle by his side, knife in hand, and a dead bear's teeth closed around his lacerated jugular.   But this is not the story you wish to hear to-night.

"I had heard something of the haunted gorge, from the lips of old trappers and hunters, who had come down to Grand Rapids in the spring to dispose of their winter spoils. But as such stories were common around the lodge fires, and were always listened to by the younger men with an honest belief that the most extravagant exaggeration could not impair, I listened to them only for the amusement of an idle hour. But as one or two men of hardier judgment, more truthful, and of less vivid imagination, solemnly assured me that they had personally been confronted by the spectre, I became interested in the question, and resolved to embrace the first opportunity to seek an introduction to the supposed apparition.

" The season I came out here with old LeClerc, we built our lodge within a mile of the haunt of the dreaded spectre, and the second morning after our arrival we shouldered our rifles, uncoupled our hounds, and started for the gorge. I observed that the face of the old man wore a serious and troubled look, and that not a single profane expression had broken from his lips during the entire morning. I verily believe that but for fear of having his established bravery questioned, which was his only pride, he would have flatly refused to have accompanied me in what must turn out either a silly or a frightful adventure. But the old hunter had the natural weakness of men of our calling and habits, and as he bore the conceded reputation of 'fearing neither man or devil,' to flinch now from the side of a comrade, in dread of a ghost, would furnish a text for ridicule around all the camp-fires along the lake shore.

"As soon as we reached the entrance of the gorge, the hounds broke out in full cry, and went in on a run. A herd of five deer had not been a half hour ahead of us. Le-Clerc at once caught the excitement so natural to the occasion, and with a shout of encouragement to the hounds, sprang past me, and with rapid step pushed forward upon the trail.

" The first excitement of the chase over, my attention was attracted to the strange features of the place we were treading. The sides were almost perpendicular, while high above us the mighty hemlocks leaned over the abyss, their mingled tops forming so close a cover, that not one ray of sunshine could break in upon the solemn gloom by which we were enshrouded. Of course it was the fever of imagination, but I *did* fancy that I felt the fanning of invisible wings in the motionless air, and a rank, graveyard odor seemed to ooze out from the sides of the gorge, and to rise up from the mouldering, rotten vegetation into which our feet sank at every step. I had heard of the valley and the shadow of death, and here seemed the fearful realization of it in the wilderness, and upon the earth.

" To tell the truth, a fear to which I had heretofore been a stranger, began to usurp possession of my faculties. But the old man had become so absorbed in the hunt, and in listening to the baying of the dogs, that he seemed to have entirely forgotten all his previous misgivings, his present surroundings of a superstitious nature, and began to let loose his restrained profanity with prodigal volubility.

" He had just delivered himself of a shocking malediction against a hidden root, over which he had stumbled, when a low, whimpering cry was heard a short distance ahead, and a moment thereafter both dogs came bounding toward us, shivering in an agony of fear, and crouched down behind Le-Clerc, who was about a dozen yards in advance of where I stood. The old man, who had been closely observing the trail from the time of our first entering, raised his eyes at this singular action of his petted and favorite animals, and looked straight ahead in the direction from which they had so unexpectedly come.

"I shall never fully free my vision from the scene which followed this sudden action of the old hunter. In an instant he stood as one petrified. His rifle dropped from his hand and rattled against a stone. I could not see his eyes, but I knew that some horrible fascination had riveted their gaze. I hastened to his side as fast as the little power of motion left me would permit. He raised his right arm slowly from his side, pointed up the gorge, and sank down upon the ground.

"I looked in the direction indicated. About a hundred feet in advance, between two dead hemlock trees, stood a figure completely enveloped in a black shroud. It was motionless, but erect. The outlines were unmistakably human. Strange to say, my terror had in a measure left me the moment the object was discerned, and my faculties of observation seemed rather sharpened than impaired. I tried every mode of reasoning that would assist to the belief that what I saw was rather an illusion than a reality. It would not do. The dreadful apparition was too palpable, too well-defined, too distinct from the nature of all of its surroundings, to be classed with any real substance. Even as I looked, it sank slowly into the ground, then as slowly rose up to its former proportions; a shadowy arm protruded through the shroud, pointed to a spot on the side of the precipice close to the floor of the gorge, the arm slowly shrank back beneath its covering, and then the object gradually melted away and was gone!

"I looked around upon my companion. He was sitting up, and had evidently witnessed all that I had myself seen. His face was very pale, but a more subdued expression by far was upon his features than I had ever seen there before. At last he said:

"'Comrade, we will not now talk about what we have just witnessed. Let us return. To-morrow we will come here again, and examine the spot to which the spirit pointed. Take your hatchet and blaze this tree. Then we shall be certain of the place.'

"Neither of us had any appetite for supper that night, and the small hours of the morning were upon us ere we ventured to seek repose in sleep. The dogs lay stretched before the fire, but were as wakeful as their masters, whining piteously at intervals, as though disturbed by some invisible intruder.

"But the weary hours of the night dragged their slow length along, and the wished for day dawned at last. A few mouthfulls of cold venison, eaten without appetite, sufficed for our breakfast, and the sun was just coming up out of the east as we started on our journey to try to investigate the ghostly mystery of the previous day. We walked on, slowly and in silence, over the intervening mile. The 'blazed' tree was soon found, and then we approached the two old hemlocks, between whose dead trunks the vision had been discovered.

"I stepped at once to the spot on the side of the precipice to which it had pointed, and commenced the examination. Nothing unusual was to be seen, from the first curious glance we cast around. We were beginning to look upon the affair as a delusion, or some natural phenomenon that had deceived our heated senses, and I commenced joking LeClerc about our childish fancies. But to be more fully satisfied on this point, I turned my face toward the dead hemlocks, to see if we had the right range of the spot toward which the spectre had pointed.

"And there it stood again, right within ten feet of us, its shrouded figure so clearly defined, as to remove all doubt of the perfection of our senses! I touched my comrade upon the arm. He looked up, and his eyes followed the direction of my own. Even as we stood, in breathless silence, and gazed in awe, a shadowy arm gradually protruded from the shroud, and pointed to the spot upon which we stood!

"It is strange, but neither of us were in the least shaken with fear. A solemn sense of some dread, but unknown duty devolving upon us, was the only sensation by which we were affected.

"In a few moments the spectre slowly faded away, as on the day previous. Then LeClerc took the muzzle of his rifle and parted the low bushes, and matted vines, that had grown out of the side of the slope, where it rested on the bottom of the gorge. And then the discovery was made.

"The mouth of a cave, about twenty inches in diameter, right in front of which, and pressing against it, was the body of a young hemlock, of about a dozen years growth. A quantity of decayed branches, leaves, &c., partially filled the mouth of the cavern, and these, with the tree in front, interfered with our explorations. But we had our hatchets with us, and it took but a few minutes to bring the tree to the ground. The accumulated rubbish was easily removed, and the feet and skull of a ghastly human skeleton were revealed! A pair of pantaloons, and a shirt, still clothed the rest of the skeleton in their rotten folds. A hat lay on the bottom of the cave. On examining this, we discovered a piece of paper inside, which had evidently been torn from the inner lining of the hat. On this was written with a pencil the following, which we found but little difficulty in deciphering, the cave being of sandy formation, and removed from all damp surroundings. The lines read thus:

" ' I know that I am dying, and I feel that an angry God is here. In my life I scoffed at His name, and derided His promises and His threatenings. In my dying hour He has closed his mercy against me. Hope is gone forever, and a black eternity opens before me. Should my remains be discovered, the prayer of a dying wretch is, that they may be removed to the burying grounds of some Christian church.

" ' January, 1851.'

" Upon after inquiry, I learned that in the same month of the same year a vessel had been wrecked on the coast near by the gorge, and it was supposed that all hands had perished. There is little doubt that one of the passengers had reached the shore, wandered into the uninhabited wilderness, and finally crept into this cave, and perished of cold and exhaustion.

" We left the skeleton precisely as we had found it, and returned to camp. After supper we discussed the matter between us, and agreed upon a plan of action. There was a little log Methodist Church at Pentwater, about twelve miles distant, and we resolved to start with the remains the next day, and comply with the last request of the unhappy stranger.

" In the morning we found it impossible to get material to make a box, and so we took one of our blankets, went back to the cave, carefully removed the skeleton, wrapped it up in the blanket, carried it to the beach, deposited it in our log canoe, and rowed for Pentwater.

" It was growing dark when we reached our destination, for the lake was up in its wrath, and what little headway we could make was amid the greatest dangers. We saw no one on our way to the little graveyard, for it was some considerable distance from the half dozen huts that composed the settlement. With our paddles we soon dug a hole of sufficient depth in the sandy soil, deposited the remains, and covered them from sight. Then the old man grasped me by the hand, and said:

" 'Comrade, I need not tell you that I have been a very wicked man, and of violent deeds and of blaspheming tongue. What you and me have recently witnessed, is a warning from Heaven to us both. Henceforth and forever I renounce my evil ways, so far as grace is given me to resist temptation, and I know that prayer is mighty and will prevail. Let us pray for the dead.'

"And we kneeled down upon the new made grave of the stranger, and the old man poured forth a fervent supplication, with a sincerity of soul that I fear is seldom heard in the great churches of your eastern cities. And then we arose and departed for our boat, better men than we had ever been before.

" I never heard a profane word from the lips of LeClerc afterward, nor even a momentary ebullition of anger at any trivial annoyance. And his changed deportment had a wonderful influence upon the rude men of the wilderness, with whom he associated, for they knew there was none of the sham of hypocrisy in the rough old French hunter. That is a vice that only pays where there is 'refined society.'

" And now," said the hunter, after a short pause, and turning his clear honest blue eyes full upon my face, " of course you don't believe my strange story. I cannot ask you to. I would not believe it myself, had it been told me by another.

" And yet," he added, after musing a few moments, " the human mind, in the learned or ignorant, the profane as well as the pious, is always moved to either clear or doubtful credulity at stories of the supernatural. And how can there be belief in that which is *impossible?* There can be no superstructure, material or spiritual, without *foundation.* Therefore I hold that the mere fact that our race, savage, barbaric, or christianized, all have their superstitions, is proof positive of a Divine cause that produces this universal effect. I go further and say that all of mental action is from God. That man may pervert and misdirect is another question. But there can be no superstition without a reality for its basis. If the dead do not live again we could not think they do."

The hour was now late, and we retired. It was long before sleep broke in upon the meditations which the hunter's story had set in action.

Dear reader, there are more things in Heaven and Earth than are dreamed of in your philosophy.

MY MOTHER.

'TIS but a week ago to-day
　　My mother passed from earth;
I cannot weep, I cannot pray,
　　Yet never grief had sadder birth.

Adown the gloom of weary years,
　　My pilgrim memory takes its way;
It passes shrines bedewed with tears,
　　Forgotten till this judgment day.

I see a little head at rest—
　　A little baby boy in sleep
Upon a youthful mother's breast,
　　Whose joy is voiceless deep.

Again the shadows slowly lift,
　　From out the gloom of the dead years,
And where the sunlight throws its drift,
　　That boy, a man appears.

And sin and shame is on his brow,
　　A lifeless life of crime and wrong;
Forgot, or broken every vow
　　He learned in cradle song.

O! mother, to thy hairs of gray
　　Thy child brought little else than grief;
God pity those who thus repay
　　The love beyond belief!

And here, all stripped of passion's power,
　　I kneel beside thy new-made grave,
And plead His grace—O! sacred dower!—
　　The grace to bless and save!

Send earthward from Thy holy throne
　　The balm that saves the soul from pain—
Bereft, sad, penitent, *alone*—
　　Let child and mother meet again!

THE "OLD SETTLER" GOES TO CHURCH IN FULL DRESS.

————•—————

IT had been announced that on the following Sabbath a sermon would be preached in our little school-house, and so unusual an event created no little stir among the few settlers of the Ridge. The matrons hunted up the old fashioned linen caps that they had brought with them from their old homes, and which had been carefully laid away against the day of possible need. The young women did their level best, you bet, with the scanty material at hand, to add to their natural attractions. The men looked ruefully at their patched solitary suits, of a style belonging to a past rustic generation, and meditated, with indecision, as to whether it were better to sacrifice the little remaining pride of personal appearance, to their desire to see the preacher, and to hear the "sarmint."

I had requested of the "Old Settler" that he would accompany me on the occasion, and assured him that it would afford me great pleasure to attend under his escort.

"Durn it, mister," was his response, "don't be a pokin' fun at a feller. Look here, how about goin' to meetin' in sich trousers?"

As he said this, he turned slowly around, and with his finger directed my attention to about a score of patches, of as many different colors.

I had a curiosity to see how the man would deport himself at a religious meeting, and to hear his after comments upon the services. And so I informed him that I had a pair of tolerably good pantaloons that I would give him, but feared they would prove much too short for his style of legs.

"That don't make a mite of difference," he rejoined, "ony so as they aint patched. I don't mind a patch or two on the seat, or on the knees, for everybody here hez to wear them kind. But when a feller's trousers is *all* patches, somehow he hates to go to a place where most everybody else hez on better clothes. Leastwise I do, and I'll be durned ef I kin git over it. I know poor folks oughtn't be proud, but human nater *will* go agin what it oughtn't to."

Noticing that his shirt hung in rags, and having some unbleached muslin in the house, I proffered him sufficient for that article, provided he thought his wife could manage to make it up for him in time for the meeting.

To my surprise the man manifested genuine feeling at this proposition, and the tears came to his eyes, as in a subdued voice he exclaimed :

"Durn it, mister, you'm a leetle too good to such a mean cuss as I am. I know'd them taters wuz froze when I sold 'em to you, and ever since then I've kinder tried to git the best of you, for I sort of felt that you couldn't help but believe that I wuz an ornary rascal. But we hadn't a pound of meat, nor of flour—only a quart or two of ingin—in the cabin, and not a cent to buy enny with. That boss in the lumber camp run away with all our winter airnin's, and what could a poor feller like me do ? That's why the devil put it into my head to sell you them taters, which they got froze because the wind blowed the snow off of the place where they wuz buried. And when a man hez done a mean thing, and knows it, he tries to bully it out, as though he wuz right, and tries to make himself believe it, though its the durnd'est hardest job ever a feller undertook. And now that I hev owned up to that blasted tater business, I feel better, and more like a man, and ef there wuz ony enny preachin' goin' on right here, durn'd ef I don't b'lieve that I should git right down on my knees, and pray of the good Lord to fergive me of my sins."

Somewhat astounded at this blunt and unexpected confession, I looked searchingly into the man's face; but its expression confirmed all that he had said. The hard, rigid lines, the bold, defiant glance, in which courage was so mingled with cunning, had all been softened down in a moment to a look of penitence and remorse. The better nature of this buffeted and hardened being had obtained a momentary mastery, and the image of God was vindicated in this seemingly most reckless and abandoned of His creatures. He hung his head, and a few big tears rolled down his bronzed and weather-beaten cheeks. Was this a passing emotion, a transient gleam of the purity of our race before sin entered Eden, and defiled the shrine of the Divinity with which the Creator had endowed the creature? Or was it the permanent lifting up of the lost and degraded to his original statue before the Master, which Christ promised to all who would confess their sins and put their burdens upon him?

I found myself unable to respond to what this uncouth being had so earnestly uttered, so strange had his altered manner affected and confounded me. I entered the house, obtained the pantaloons, an old vest, and a few yards of muslin, returned and handed the articles to him. He received them in an humble and thankful manner, and without saying a word, walked away slowly, with bowed head, in the direction of his cabin.

How many wretches there are, who are nearer the Kingdom than the judgment of even good men is willing to admit! O! ye of little faith!

About nine o'clock on the next Sabbath morning, a man was seen coming toward our cabin, whose appearance at first defied all my efforts at recognition, and alarmed the female portion of the household. But when he reached the house, and uttered his "good mornin', mister," the "Old Settler" stood revealed before us. It was just all we could do to restrain our laughter, and little Alice ran indoors, and then fairly screamed with mirth. The man had on his gift pantaloons, which were fully eight inches too short for him, and fitted so tightly to his huge limbs, that it seemed as if his legs had been melted and run therein. There was a space of about four inches between the top of his pantaloons and vest. On his right foot he had a large cavalry boot, and on the other a low shoe, the heel of which showed a determination to run outward and turn upward.

But that new shirt! O, for the pen of a Dr. McCosh! As it is, my description must be tame. It swelled out at the bosom like a balloon, and a roll, resembling a huge yellowish life preserver, bulged out from the neutral ground between said vest and said pantaloons. The collar, heavily creased, unstarched, hid nearly the entire of his head, while the points came around in dangerous proximity to his eyes. The thought suggested itself that he must have put that shirt on wrong end up! And all this bodily grotesqueness of apparel was crowned with the beautiful new stovepipe hat he had captured from me, on the occasion before described in these pages!

The "Old Settler" scanned each face before him quickly, and saw the evidence of restrained mirth. His subdued expression of the day before had lost much of its humility, still his old assurance was not there. If his heart was as changed as his face, he had become a comparatively Christian man. Our furtive scrutiny of his dress abashed him but for a moment, and then with one eye partly closed, and a humorous twinkle playing around the other, he asked :

"Mister, how do I look ?"

"Like an emperor," I responded. " When we first saw you coming over the hill, we all thought it must be the minister."

" Well," he rejoined, in a good natured tone, "I don't blame you folks for makin' a little fun of the old man. I ruther guess I *do* look purty durn'd curious. But it tuk me and the old woman a good hour to git this riggin' on, ennything like ship shape. And then she laid right down on the floor and laughed, and laughed, and laughed, as ef she would die, which I almost hoped she would, and between laughs she axed me not to go a cavortin' around among the gals, and thus break the heart of so good a wife as she had been unto me for nigh upon forty years past. But, mister, I done the best I could, which the things didn't fit me nohow, and ef you would ruther not go with me to the meetin', lookin' as I do, jist say so, and I will go by myself, and no hard thoughts agin you."

I hastily assured the " Old Settler " that the thought at which he hinted had no place in my mind, and invited him into the cabin. As soon as we were seated, with an effort that threatened disaster to his new pantaloons, he crossed his cavalry leg over the other, and said :

"Mister, this ere boot is all the plunder that I brought back with me out of the war, when I fout under Old Sharman. I was on picket the day arter the beautiful scrimmage at Missionary Ridge, when I seed a crow sailin' round and round over a little bunch of bushes, about thirty rod from where I stood watchin' some rebel horsemen, away over on the ridge of a hill. Well, I went over to them bushes, which it wuz agin orders, but I wanted to see what that crow meant. And there, sure enough, laid a rebel officer, flat on his face, dead. There was no sword in his scabbard, and no money in his pockets, which I sarched for the sake of his family. But he hed on a good pair of new boots, and I wuz about barefoot. And so I tuk hold of one of 'em, and after tuggin' mighty hard for five minutes, which the leg was swelled, I managed to git *that* boot off. Then I tackled the other, but I couldn't budge it a mite. I seed that a cannon ball had knocked the knee of this leg all to flinders, and so the poor feller, which he was a big, good looking chap, had managed to crawl into the bushes and die. Well, I yanked away at that tother boot, for I guess fifteen minutes, without gainin' a mite on it. At last, fur I expected the Relief every minute, I gin it an almighty jerk, and the hull thing cum off at the knee, sendin' me head foremost onto the ground!

"Well, mister, I hed no corkscrew, you know, and so I hed to leave that boot, which was a shame. I daren't take it into camp with the leg in it, for the boys would hev give me some durn'd nickname about it, which I never would hear the last of.

"But it wuz jist my luck, fur everything has seemed to go agin me, from the time I wuz a little boy. But I held on to tother boot, all through Tenesee, Georgee, North Carliny, clear to Pottymax Court House, and at last brought it home with me. I hev never wore it afore to-day, only wunst when I went to 'lection to wote fur Old Greeley. Folks sed he ony wore one boot, and that's the why I woted fur him."

The time to move for the meeting had now arrived, and we started, leaving the rest of the family, who were decidedly averse to close companionship with the "Old Settler" on this occasion, to follow at a respectful distance. Arrived at the school-house, we found about forty people assembled, anxious for the appearance of the preacher. Among them were a number of strangers from the mills, a much better paid and better clothed class than any of the permanent settlers. The moment my companion entered and took his seat, a general giggle went around the assembly. The mill men were particularly demonstrative, and scanned my companion's dress with broad grins, and insulting gestures of supercilious superiority. The old man noticed this at once, and his face, determined at all times in its expression, darkened with anger. At last he leaned over to me and whispered:

"Neighbor, as soon as the sarvice is over, I'm a goin' to shake up two or three of them durn'd Yankee mill fellers to see ef there is enny manners in 'em. I mean to shake 'em good—so they will stay shook ontil the next preacher comes along."

He then raised his huge fist, and brought it down three times, with a heavy "thug" upon his knee, looking hard at the offenders all the while. The insulting demonstrations instantly ceased. All the country round knew that "Pete Higgins" was a dangerous man to be lightly trifled with; for in strength, activity, and courage, he had no equal in the entire county, and he never calculated the odds, when fully aroused by insult or injustice.

It was fifteen minutes past the time when the preacher arrived. As he entered and stepped upon the low platform, the whole audience was at once hushed into silence—the silence of awe. There appeared before them a man over six feet in stature, erect, thin in features, long, white hair that fell down upon his shoulders, and a port and bearing such as is ascribed to one born to command. His large, eager, black eyes gleamed with a strange light that seemed not of earth, and appeared to emit a holy, confident defiance against an ungodly world in arms. If there ever was a man fearless of martyrdom, that apostle of faith was now before us.

L

"Friends," he commenced, in a low, sweet tone, of almost womanly tenderness, "I am seventy years old this day, and find that at last I have miscalculated my strength. I walked from Pentwater (twelve miles distant) this morning, to meet you here, and became wearied by the way. The spirit was willing but the flesh was weak. God tries his servants, and his enemies, alike by the same physical laws. My limbs are not as lithe as in the years that are past. But the strength that is left to me shall be cheerfully spent in His service— *glory to His great name!* Let us pray."

The preacher, with both arms extended, stood erect, but every head in his presence was bowed as by a common impulse. And then, in a low, solemn voice, he prayed:

"God of all space; God of the wilderness; God of the waste places, where no man is; God of the city full, where sin flaunts its disregard of Thee even in Thy temples, soften *my* heart, and the hearts of these Thy neglected *children*, that they may be opened to the admission of Thy spirit, and Thy grace abound therein, even as the waters fill the limits of the great deep. Let not the rod of Moses be weakened in the centuries of sin, and shame, and crime; for there are hearts now, even here, whose waters are sealed as with adamant, and Thy power alone can cause them to flow forth to vivify for eternity the graces and the glories of redeemed mortality. God of all, Saviour of those who will, Sanctifier of the blessed who die in the Lord, show Thy power through Thy servant this day, unto this people, and the glory shall be unto the Giver of every good and perfect gift—*Amen!*"

The preacher was not heard in his prayer for "much speaking," but that moment there were live coals upon rude altars, that had perhaps never felt the glow of a religious emotion before. Faces, unwonted in solemnity, revealed the thoughts that had startled the soul within. The people had listened to a *prayer*, instead of an *affectation*. God is only with the word when the utterer is with God.

Then the old apostle took from his pocket a well worn book, and read out a hymn. Finding that none of his audience could assist in that comforting part of the service, he sang the selection alone, in so earnest and touching a manner, that even those who neither comprehended its words or sentiments, were affected by an inspiration of the emotions into a sort of religious appreciation that was depicted plainly in their faces. For myself, I had never heard the hymn before, but well do I now remember one recurring line :

"Jesus of Nazareth passeth by."

But I have listened to it since, and rendered in such low, soft, sweet melody, as to thrill my soul almost into harmony with the spirits of just men made perfect.

Then the preacher announced his text : "*The poor have the gospel preached unto them.*"

I have heard very many pulpit discourses in my day, from the wordy lips of the religious demagogues of the Beecher school, who in the motto of the shopkeeper, "study to please," to the zealous fanatic who rants shockingly about sublime truths which his shallow brain is incapable of comprehending, and who approaches God more as a familiar than as a worshipper. But never until this day had I heard a preacher who came so near the ideal standard of my conception of what a dispenser of the Word should strive to attain to. There was none of those painfully disgusting exhibitions of vanity—of *self*—peeping out of studied oratorical sentences, now so common with the clergy of our blinded and self-deceived congregations. As friend talks to friend, earnest for his welfare, did this man, his eyes fixed first upon one listener, and then another, speak of the Redeemer of the race, his sinless sufferings for the sins of others, ending in the most horrible of deaths. He told his hearers how Christ, leaving the unjust of wealth, and the powerful of oppression, to their own ways, went among the lowly and the despised, bound up the broken hearted, and lifted the soul of the beggar up to the inheritance of an eternity ever glorious in immortality, that all the potentates of earth could neither give nor take away. Standing there, his tall form dilating in his fervent passion, his large eyes emitting magnetic flashes that held in the bonds of wonder, fear, and amazement, the most stupid listener, he seemed the risen personification of the great Apostle of the Gentiles. Toward the close, unwearied in effort, and unflagging in utterance, he stepped from the platform, walked down among the people, raised the little children in his arms and kissed them, laid his hands upon the heads of hardened, stalwart men and blessed them, while his exhortations, so full of touching pathos for the welfare of others, shed a holy influence upon all present, and sobs and groans from hearts that had never uttered them before, attested a power greater than that of man.

At the close of the meeting, which lasted nearly two hours, the strange preacher, of whom no man present knew ought, prepared to depart. He refused all invitations to dinner, and to remain over night, stating that he stood in need of neither food nor shelter then, and that the Lord would provide against the hour of his necessity. With a parting blessing, he again walked forth into the wilderness, another John the Baptist, upon his mission.

I had become so wholly absorbed in the wonderful utterances of the strange preacher, that I had forgotten to observe the effect upon the "Old Settler" up to this time. When I at last looked for him, I discerned that he had left the room, and was standing some distance from the door, his back towards us, rubbing an old, ragged fragment of a handkerchief, in a hasty and impatient manner, over his eyes and face. He had evidently been weeping, and was trying to obliterate this evidence of his weakness.

Just then the mill men started in a body on their way home. The " Old Settler " turned around upon them, and confronting the leader, said :

" Mister, you had ought'er hev thanked thet preacher, afore he went away. He hez saved you from one of the durnd'est lickin's ever a Yankee got in these parts."

The old man maintained his half defiant attitude for a few moments, as though anxious that his adversary would make some demonstration that would release him from the moral resolution he had formed, under the effect of the preaching, to forgive the previous insults. But to our surprise the "yankee," who was evidently a sensible man, and of kindly feelings, asked pardon for his thoughtless offence, and declared that he was sorry for it.

" Durn my pictur ! durn everybody ! " exclaimed the "Old Settler," as he wheeled around out of the path, his eyes again flushed with tears, " ef I aint a gittin' to be a great blubberin' baby, who is ashamed of hisself ! "

And thus speaking, he joined me and we started homeward. We had walked some little distance in silence, when my companion, ridding himself of a deep sigh, said :

" Mister, I aint as big a fool as you think I am. This hat is yourn. I know'd you didn't intend to give it to me about them bugs. But I thought it a good chance to git the better of you agin, and so I tuk it. It's jist as the preacher says. When a man does one mean thing, the devil is always on hand to coax him to foller it up.

" And," he continued, after a brief pause, and another

sigh, "I wish I was dead, ony I aint fit. I owe you ten dollars fur them taters, which was froze, and five more dollars, borrered money. Now I've got a heffer, which she will come in next spring. She aint got hardly enny flesh onto her bones, but she's wuth all of fifteen dollars. She's yourn."

I assured my companion that nothing could induce me to accept his proposition, and that I could afford to lose all he owed me, without the least inconvenience. At any rate he must not think of paying me until he was abundantly able.

"I know what you mean," said the "Old Settler," you want me to feel easy like, ez if I hedn't done ennything much wrong. Thet won't do. The preecher told me what God expects a man to do what has cheated his neighbor. He sed we must pay back agin four fold. Thet I *can't* do. Well, then, what I *kin* do, comes next. Mister, don't let your good natur' make you talk what ain't right. A bad feller kin find excuses enough fur his wickedness, without hevin' tolerably good folks, who know better, tryin' to help him cheat *them* and *hisself* too."

I felt sorely rebuked at this unexpected logic, from this awakened man—awakened to new ideas of his responsibility to Deity—and before I could collect my thoughts for a response, he struck a by-path that led to his cabin, and soon disappeared in the woods.

I arose early the next morning, and on opening the door of my cabin, there, upon the head of a barrel, was my new hat! After breakfast I went down to the barn, and there, lying by the side of my own two beautiful calves, "Hagar" and "Daisy," was the poor, thin heifer of the "Old Settler!"

In the night he had come and made all the restitution in his power! How many of the "converted" sinners of our city churches have ever done the same?

I intend to keep that animal, pet and feed her well, and when she "comes in," next spring, the wife of the "Old Settler" shall have her as a present, if it is in my power to effect such purpose. The result will be made known in my next volume.

TO MY LITTLE SPARROW.

POOR little birdie, with feathers so brown,
How do you feel when the snow comes down,
With its wintry mantle all over the town?
"Chip!" "chip!"

And the wind whistles wild round every corner,
And you so unlike little Jack Horner,
Who had a snug place in the chimney corner?
"Chip!" "chip!"

Dear little bird, to my window sill come,
For while my cupboard has in it a crumb,
I will fast myself, but you shall have some.
"Chip!" "chip!"

From the dark clouds above the white drift is tossed,
And thy poor little body is pinched with the frost,
Yet the hope that God gave thee can never be lost!
"Chip!" "chip!"

The days are now near when thy little brown wing
Will be spread, mid the beauty and odor of Spring,
And thy heart its new birth of enjoyment will sing,
"Chip!" "chip!"

Teach me, little bird, to be strong against fate,
To see through the storms of my earthly estate,
The sunshine that gleams through the Heavenly gate!
"Chip!" "chip!"

MY ANGEL.

TO THEE, O, God! I lift my rescued soul,.
   In holiest praise,
To bless Thee for the saving hope vouchsafed
   My later days.

When all was but as darkest frowning night,—
   No kindling beam
Threw o'er the weary waste of a long life,
   One cheering gleam.

Swift to the gulf of my unblest despair
   An angel came,
And bending o'er the fearful, dark abyss,
   Whispered my name!

Then in my leprous heart a glory shone
   At Thy command,
And through the darkness of my fate I saw,
   My angel's hand!

Safe to the Rock she lifted up my feet
   From sensual mire,
And purified my former evil thoughts
   From base desire!

Immortal Spirit! bless this angel bright,
   So dear to me,
Who lifted from my soul eternal night,
   And bade me see!

TO THE READER.

MY DEAR FRIEND:—You, individually. My first effort in the book line is before you, (or rather behind you now)—either for condemnation, approval, or a mixed sentiment of both feelings. It is no hypocritical, self-depre-cating utterance, which holds hidden vanity, when I assure you that I am not proud of the performance. That the work was not undertaken from high moral considerations, or a desire to add to the instructive productions of the day, or to exalt the tone of public literature, is evident from the careless, hap-hazard, contradictory tone that permeates most of the enclosed pages. My object was to make a little money, not from a mercenary consideration, but because misfortune created necessity. I could have made more money, and made it easier, by editing a Grant newspaper ; *but then, what does it profit a man if he gain the whole world and lose his own soul!* Your author—thanks to the good Lord who enabled him, in all his life of recklessness, to retain a fair reputation for at least personal honesty—is neither a Congressional Credit Mobilier villain, or a low back pay grabber. In other words, he is not an " Honorable," who professed extra purity for the opportunity of manifesting extra putridity. As this is about the only trait of character I have to boast of, you will pardon me for keeping it rather ostentatiously to the front.

From such a character, therefore, you could expect little else than common-place, either in morals pious, or morals pecuniary.

That I have not, in these pages, outraged a religious sentiment, or offended reasonable delicacy, is all that any one,
who knew me by my past life, had a right to expect. And
in what I have within written, this negative virtue is all of
which I am congratulatory proud. To conquer a lifelong
habit of thought and expression, is a victory of hopeful import, under the proverb that it is "hard to teach old dogs
new tricks!"

Compact the time in which this book was written, and the
sum total will not reach ten days. Neither plan nor plot
was studied or contemplated, and all herein contained flowed
from a pen that was unaware of its design, and pursued its
course as unpremeditated thought pushed it upon its journey.
A disjointed medley, and an unsatisfactory whole, is the verdict of the writer's own judgment. If the reader rises from
the perusal with a more generous estimate, then I am amply
paid for my efforts in such reader's behalf—*your own little
dollar, now snugly in my pocket, being attached to the moral
consideration.* Without that addenda, it is possible that my
estimate of your appreciation might lack the heartiness which
recognizes the "cheerful giver." Personification of unselfish-
ness as your author is, he has the modified weakness of his
tribe for the root that is said to foundation all evil. The
man who vaunts his disregard of "filthy lucre," be he priest
or layman, the same is a liar of the grandest magnitude, and
the truth is not in him. As this blow hits all around, the
established impartiality of my character is not injuriously
affected by this parting swing of the cudgel.

And now, dear reader, man or woman, we part right here
for the present. If this little book of mine, neither harmful
or useful, which I sent unto you with so much doubt of its
reception, meets with a favor beyond my own estimate of its
merits, then will you have conferred upon me a delight hardly

hoped for, and in consequence so much the more gratefully received and cherished. And the immediate aggressive result will be (for unexpected success makes one presumptuous,) the taxing of this poor brain of mine for another volume of an entirely different texture from the unfledged bantling you are now closing from perusal. And so, with an honest, heartfelt blessing upon you and yours, now, and in the unexplored hereafter, receive my affectionate "good bye!"